The Death of a King

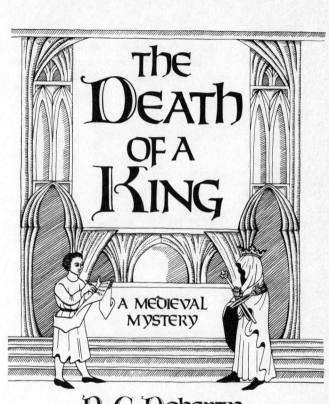

THE DEATH OF A KING

A MEDIEVAL MYSTERY

P. C. Doherty

St. Martin's Press
New York

Library of Congress Cataloging in Publication Data

Doherty, P. C.
    The death of a king.

    1. Great Britain—History—Edward II-III, 1307-1377—
Fiction.   I. Title.
PR6054.037D4   1986   823'.914   85-25123
ISBN 0-312-18651-7

First published in Great Britain by Robert Hale Ltd.

Foreword

The history of fourteenth-century England is full of tales of terror, war, intrigue and betrayal. Often it is difficult to distinguish between fact and fiction. We can only look at events and speculate on the variety of causes behind them. This applies to the horrifying revelations contained in this collection of letters.

However, to assist the reader, I have included a list of the main historical personages mentioned in the text. The list does not include those mysterious, sinister figures who lived, worked and died in the shadowy world surrounding the great and famous of Europe.

P.C. Doherty, 1982

Historical Personages

EDWARD I   King of England, 1272–1307.

EDWARD II   King of England, 1307–1327.

ISABELLA   Wife of Edward II and Queen of England from 1308 to her retirement in 1330.

EDMUND, EARL OF KENT   Half-brother to Edward II, executed 1329.

THOMAS, EARL OF LANCASTER   Cousin to Edward II and the king's life-long opponent. Defeated and executed by Edward II in 1322.

JOHN STRATFORD   Bishop of Winchester, then Archbishop of Canterbury.

ADAM ORLETON   Bishop of Hereford. Later Bishop of Worcester.

ROGER MORTIMER OF WIGMORE   Welsh baron, opponent of Edward II. He escaped to France, where he joined with queen Isabella in 1325. They invaded England, deposed Edward II and ruled England until Mortimer's overthrow in 1330.

EDWARD III   King of England, 1327–1377. Edward II's successor and son of Queen Isabella.

Letter One

Edward, by the grace of God, King of England, France and Ireland, to Our faithful clerk, Edmund Beche, health and greetings. We command you to meet Us at Windsor on the first Sunday after the Assumption to discuss a matter touching Our Crown. It is Our royal pleasure and your duty to attend. Under no circumstances will We excuse your absence.
Written at Westminster and despatched under the secret seal,
10 August 1345.

Edmund Beche to his faithful friend, Richard Bliton, Prior of Croyland Abbey, health and blessing. It is a long time Richard, since we studied together at Oxford, yet our friendship seems to have stood the test of time and changing personal fortune. You are the prior of a great abbey but I, now 35, continue to scratch away as a clerk in the royal Chancery. True, I have no great desire to change. My fees suffice to provide robes, food, a sound horse, a house in Bread Street and a pert young woman in Cheapside. Should the latter offend your 'holiness' then I apologize but, unlike you, I have no vocation to remain celibate or, like so many, worsen my state by matrimony.

The writ I enclose from our king, Edward III, now

threatens my humdrum existence. A royal messenger delivered it with all the arrogance he could muster on the morning of 12 August, and small and terse though it is, the writ caused me great concern. As far as I knew, I had done nothing wrong, but you can never be sure. Some of my work in the writing office of the Chancery deals with royal correspondence of varying degrees of secrecy. If ale had made me loquacious in some Holborn tavern, then perhaps my comfortable existence was going to end rather abruptly. So, from the moment I received the summons, my agitation grew and the actual journey to Windsor did little to curb my anxiety.

The bells of St Paul's were clanging for Sunday Prime when a mailed clatter outside my lodgings rattled me awake. I pushed open a casement to find a courtier whom I knew by sight, Sir John Chandos, and a group of sergeants wearing the blue and gold of the royal livery staring up at me. Sir John, tall, grey-haired, with a face like a hunting falcon, was courteous but firm. The king, he shouted, wanted me at Windsor and I was to accompany him there immediately. I dressed swiftly in my best robes and hurried down to join him. I was grateful that the problem of how I was to meet the king had now solved itself, but worried sick over why a military escort had been sent to take me. We marched down to Queenhithe's wharf where a barge, flying the golden leopards of England and the silver fleur-de-lis of France, lay waiting. We clambered in, the order was given to cast off and soon we were in mid-stream, rowing north through the swirling morning mist.

Apart from the splash of the dipping oars, the journey was a quiet one. I did not question Chandos and he confined himself to a few conventional remarks about my work in the Chancery and my brief military service against the French. His presence did little to comfort me. Sir John

Chandos has a reputation as a ferocious fighter, totally devoted to a king who had elevated him from relative obscurity to be a member of his council. A mysterious figure always in the shadows, he acted as bodyguard and confidant to the king. He had been a member of that select group of retainers who had aided the king in the famous coup of 1330, which destroyed the rule of his mother and her lover Mortimer. Sir John had led the party which actually arrested Mortimer, killing in hand-to-hand combat two of the latter's bodyguards. Since then court chatter had Sir John Chandos as the paramount figure in a number of secret and dangerous assignments. Some called him a spy but others dismissed him as the king's secret and most professional assassin.

By the time we docked at Windsor, the sun was beginning to lift the morning mist but the fear twisting in the pit of my stomach kept me cold and clammy. We left the barge and headed towards the huge donjon of the great grey castle, the armour of the sergeants echoing along the rutted streets like the tambour-beat of a death march. We crossed the great yawning moat and entered the main gate. The portcullis fell with a crash. The escort was dismissed and I followed Chandos across the castle yard into the recently renovated chapel. We walked up the main aisle, genuflected before a winking sanctuary lamp and, turning left, entered a small, cool chamber which must also serve as the vestry. At the far end, two figures sat hunched over a trestle table. They looked up as we entered. Chandos ordered me to kneel and an age seemed to pass before a resonant voice told me to sit on the stool Chandos had pushed alongside me. I slumped on to it and, raising my eyes, found myself staring straight into the king's face. My first thought was that the golden boy we students cheered so wildly as he passed through Oxford to his palace at Woodstock had disappeared. The blond hair had turned a dull grey. a mottled hue of criss-crossed veins now patterned the tawny face and his belly's so big that it seems our king has lost his youth, not on the battlefield, but at the board of countless banquets. Yet his eyes, though puffy and ringed with shadows, were keen and alert enough to force me to shift my gaze to the person sitting on his left. There, I recognized the red-haired, foxy features of our father in Christ, John Stratford, Archbishop of Canterbury.

For a few moments, both Edward and his archbishop studied me. The king then leaned forward and asked if I knew my history. I replied that I had studied Polybius, Tacitus and the other ancients, which only brought neighs of laughter from Stratford.

"No, Master Beche," the king said with a half-smile, "a little more recent than that. Such as the events of my late father's reign?"

Anyone at court from porter to Earl Marshal would have sensed the danger in such a question, so I muttered a few phrases about my low station, scholarly seclusion and comparative youth when the late Edward II had been deposed and brutally murdered.

The king stirred restlessly and quickly silenced me. "Master Beche," he snapped, "if you cannot recall the events of my lamented father's reign then let me refresh your memory. My sire came to the throne in July 1307. The following January, he married Princess Isabella of France. In March 1312 I was born, then in the next eight years came my brother John of Eltham and my two good sisters, Joanna and Eleanor. My father, however, never spent much time with us. He was too involved in a constant struggle with his cousin, Thomas, Earl of Lancaster, over who would govern the realm. Despite your protests, Master Clerk," he added drily, "you probably know the outcome. In the spring of 1322, Lancaster aided by the Earl of Hereford, Roger

Mortimer and other miscreants, rose in rebellion against my father. Mortimer burnt Bridgenorth but was forced to surrender at Shrewsbury and was imprisoned in the Tower. Lancaster and Hereford fared even worse. They were trapped at Boroughbridge in Yorkshire on the river Ure. In the ensuing skirmish, Hereford died with a spear up his arse whilst Lancaster was captured and decapitated."

The king paused to drink from a pewter goblet. "My father's victory," he continued, "marked the rise of two court favourites, Hugh Despenser the Elder who became the Earl of Winchester, and his son, Hugh the Younger, also known as the Lord of Glamorgan. This precious pair virtually owned Wales, ruled my father and ruined his kingdom. My mother," the king continued as if reciting a lesson, "the queen dowager Isabella, opposed them, but to little avail. The Despensers humiliated her and she was eventually stripped of her lands and possessions."

The king leaned back, nodding at Stratford, who continued the recital in that unctuous tone reserved by leading ecclesiastics for addressing the lowly and less intelligent amongst their flock.

"In 1325 Lady Isabella and His Grace," Stratford nodded towards the king, "then only a boy of 13 summers, managed to escape to France on the pretext of being involved in certain peace negotiations. Once there, Lady Isabella refused to return and allied herself with Roger Mortimer, who had previously escaped from the Tower. To cut a long tale short, Master Clerk, the Queen received help from me and many others and invaded England. Edward II and the Despensers, being deserted by all, fled to South Wales where they were later captured."

Stratford fell silent as the king touched his arm before resuming the narrative himself.

"Look, Master Clerk. You were 20, a student at Merton

College, Oxford, when all this happened. So let us be brief. The Despensers were executed and my father deposed and imprisoned. For the next four years, Mortimer ruled the kingdom."

The king cleared his throat and fairly rushed the rest of his evidently carefully prepared speech. "Mortimer proved to be a worse tyrant than the Despensers. He had my father murdered at Berkeley Castle. He executed my uncle, Edmund, Earl of Kent, on a fictitious charge of treason and he brought my mother into disrepute. In November 1330 matters reached such a climax that I," the king paused, "that I intervened. Mortimer was arrested at Nottingham and hanged for his crimes at Tyburn. My sweet mother decided to relinquish affairs of state in order to dedicate herself to good works on her country estates."

The king stopped abruptly and ordered Chandos, who was standing at the back of the room, to serve me with wine and sweetmeats whilst he and Stratford conferred quietly together. As I ate, I realized the king had told me nothing new and omitted the more scandalous items of the story. His father was a well-known sodomite who died with a red-hot poker thrust up his arse. Isabella, the king's "sweet mother," was little better. Her ferocity had earned her the nickname of the "She-Wolf." She had, by all accounts, been Mortimer's whore, his partner in tyranny, as well as his accomplice in the murder of her husband. If it had not been for the intervention of her son, she would have certainly joined Mortimer on the scaffold. The truth is all-important, Richard, but you never tell it to princes. Especially when you sit with them and drink their wine.

Eventually, the king ceased his whispering and, turning to me, came bluntly to the point. "Master Edmund," he began, "are you wondering how events which happened so long ago affect you?" He shrugged, not waiting for an answer. "It's quite simple. I want you to investigate the circumstances surrounding my father's death. You will draw on the Exchequer, the royal treasury, to meet any expenses and receive a warrant permitting you to question anyone, as well as the right to search any records. However," the king waved an admonitory finger at me, "you must not flaunt your commission at court nor can you work amongst any records covered by the secret seal. There is nothing there touching this matter and a great deal which concerns the security of our realm in the present war against France. Finally," the king looked hard at me, "your task is to research the background of my father's death. Not, I repeat, not to hunt down his murderers. That is the task of others."

The king gulped a little more wine, raising his hand to fend off my questions, so he could continue. "I know, I know, Master Beche. Why do I want such an investigation and why do I choose you and not a group of royal commissioners? The answers are quite simple. I was only 15 when my father died. I was king in nothing but name. Mortimer controlled the realm as if it was one of his own Welsh shires. I knew nothing at the time but," the king extended his hands, "now I want to know. The dust has settled and a discreet inquiry will satisfy my curiosity. I chose you because you will observe discretion. You are a royal clerk, skilled in research and proficient in dealing with records. You have other qualities and assets which recommend you." He picked up a leaf of parchment from the table. "You are the only son of Jocelyn and Ann Beche, farmers who held land in Yorkshire. They died some time ago, but not before they saw their only son enter Merton College and emerge well qualified in the study of law. For a while, you served as a clerk in the retinue of the Earl of Montague in two campaigns against the French. On his recommendation, you were accepted into the royal

Chancery where you have distinguished yourself as a competent, industrious and, above all, discreet clerk. You have many acquaintances but no friends unless, of course," the king added wryly, "we include your mistress in Cheapside." He let the manuscript fall back on the table.

"Well," he added abruptly, "is there anything you wish to ask?"

The king's speech had surprised me but I managed to conceal my astonishment behind an obvious question. "Your grace," I blurted out, "most of the people connected with Mortimer's regime are dead, although a few are still alive." I looked as meaningfully as I could at Stratford.

"True," that old fox replied caustically, "I was in the service of Queen Isabella when Edward II died but I know nothing of the old king's death. If I did," he added firmly, "his grace would surely know of it."

I knew that Stratford was lying. He had an innate genius for survival and promotion. A friend of Lancaster, Minister under Edward II and adviser to Isabella. He had attained the pinnacle of success under Edward II, who had made him Archbishop of Canterbury. I knew he would evade any question I would ask.

So, tired of platitudes, I asked if I could question the queen dowager, but the king wearily informed me that his mother could tell me very little for she knew nothing more than she had told him already. I remembered to smile understandingly and let the matter drop, as far too dangerous to pursue.

The king pushed a small scroll towards me. "Here is your letter of commission. It does not specify your task. You will keep that secret under the pretence of writing a history of my late father's reign." As he rasped out his last order to me, Stratford's gnarled hands pushed a book of the gospels towards me. No sooner had I risen to swear myself to secrecy than Stratford gripped my wrist, forcing me to gaze into his narrow, yellow-flecked eyes. "Master Clerk," he lisped, "you will send your reports direct to the king. Your task is important, a matter of state. Divulge it and you are an attainted traitor. You do understand?"

I nodded dumbly. Stratford relaxed his grip and handed me my commission which I thrust into my belt-pouch. The king seemed a little disconcerted by his archbishop's actions and tried to cheer me with assurances and promises of support. He then deftly dismissed me and the ever-taciturn Sir John Chandos took me back to the waiting barge. He and his company took me back to Queenshithe Wharf. The journey back was sluggish against the changing tide. I hardly noticed. I sat and stared anywhere except into Chandos's cold, steel-blue eyes.

I was back in Bread Street late in the afternoon and spent the rest of the day analysing what had happened at Windsor. Why, I kept asking myself, was the king so interested in his father's death sixteen years after the event? Why the great secrecy and, above all, why had the king chosen me? True, I am a skilled civil servant with some military service but I am also a commoner, bereft of kin, few in friends and lacking any powerful patron. Facts, the king had so readily emphasised. My parents are dead, I have no kin or friends except Kate, a sweet little piece in the service of a London mercer. She swears she loves me, and probably does, but her feather brain cannot understand the simplest problem, never mind the complexities of political intrigue. In fact, I reflected bitterly, I was the type of person who quietly disappears should he anger the high and mighty. I got up from my pallet and looked into the polished metal mirror. A tired lined face stared back, sallow with large dark-ringed eyes, long thin nose and short, dark hair. I looked at myself and thought about my loneliness, the chances missed and the opportunities lost. Was I to ruin this one? Ambition and a restless excitement has persuaded me to grasp it.

Nevertheless, I am writing to you, Richard, in defiance of my lord archbishop and my forced oath of secrecy. I am not seeking advice (I beg you never to reply) but simply to entrust you with what I find. I shall tell you all, describe events and report conversations, to serve as my bond, my security against the king in the event of my disappearance or trial for treason on some trumped-up charge. All my letters, like this one, will be sent north to you by any trustworthy messenger I can find. God keep you Richard. Written at Bread Street, 16 August, 1345.

Letter Two

Edmund Beche to Richard Bliton, health and greetings. Please accept my apologies, dear friend, for the weeks that have passed since I wrote to you but the king's "secret matter" is proving to be a hard task-master.

I started the investigation in my own chambers. My absence from the Chancery went unnoticed apart from a little envious chatter, as release from normal duties usually means another step up the greasy ladder of royal preferment. I was glad to be free. Even the most dedicated clerk tires of the cramped writing quarters, the poor light, the squeak of quill on parchment and, above all, the smell of sweat and burning wax. At first, I saw my task as a holiday. I began by listing those of the present king's family and council who had survived the four-year reign of Mortimer and Isabella. My list, based on Chancery documents for the years 1326 to 1330 was long, but it soon shrank to a pitiful few. The king and Stratford claim they know little. Queen Isabella is in retirement and an unapproachable recluse, whilst the king's sisters were excluded from affairs of state on account of their youth. I also dismissed the king's present clique of friends and councillors, for they would scarcely enjoy current royal favour if they had collaborated with Mortimer. The rest of the list, the king's brother, John; his uncles, Edmund of Kent and Thomas of Norfolk; and

Edward II's gaoler, Thomas de Berkeley, are all dead.

My disappointment was acute for I had hoped my investigation would be based on personal witness. Unlike the psalmist, "I have never said in my heart all men are liars," they usually tell the truth even if it is only implicit in the lies they fabricate. I spent days and nights scrutinizing my lists, neglecting food, drink, even Kate. I was on the brink of despair when I did remember one omission from my list, Adam Orleton, Bishop of Worcester. He had been a confidant of Mortimer and his ruthless ambition became a by-word in an age notorious for its self-seeking clerics. Orleton had managed to survive Mortimer's downfall due to his episcopal office, as well as to the fact that he had only been responsible for conducting foreign policy with little influence on domestic matters. This accounted for his frequent absences from Mortimer's retinue, as well as his exclusion from the list I had first drawn up.

A few discreet inquiries amongst my colleagues revealed that after 1330, Orleton had received no further preferment. He had spent the last fifteen years in seclusion from court, ruling his diocese of Worcester like a pope. I decided to petition Orleton for assistance in writing my 'history' and was gratified by a swift reply. The bishop, so his secretary wrote, would be pleased to meet me in his chambers at Worcester Cathedral after the midday mass on the first of November, the Feast of All Saints. I left London the day after I received this reply and, after an uneventful journey, arrived in Worcester on the last day of October and lodged at an inn near the city's west gate. The next morning I went to the cathedral and presented myself to the bishop's chancellor, who led me through a maze of draughty passageways into a great chamber where Orleton was sitting enthroned behind a large oaken table. I was immediately struck by the grandeur of my surroundings: sweet-smelling rushes covered the floor whilst the walls were draped in multi-coloured tapestries from Bruges, most of them dealing with themes, certainly not to be found in the Bible or the writings of the Fathers. Around the room, beeswax candles and small glowing braziers fended off the chill November darkness. Their fire sparkled from the many precious objects which adorned the spacious chamber.

I could have stood and gawked till Christmas but when the bishop's chancellor coughed and closed the door behind me, I hastily remembered protocol. I walked forward and made the most reverent obeisance towards the desk. A harsh voice bade me stand and I rose to inspect one of England's most notorious prelates. I expected an ogre but, despite the swarth of purple robes and sable furs, the figure in the chair was frail and small and his face was as pale and finely etched as any ascetic. Yet, as Orleton leaned closer, I noticed his eyes were little, hard, black pebbles and their stare never faltered.

"You're here at the king's express command?" The voice had lost some of its sharpness.

"His grace," I replied glibly, "has commissioned me to write a history of his late father's reign. I hoped your lordship could provide me with some information concerning that king's unhappy end."

Orleton fingered a tassle on his robe. "Master Beche," he replied, "I know why you are here. The real reason, that is." He held up a scrawny, be-ringed hand to stop any denial. "I, too, have my spies, Master Clerk, so rest content with that. Let us be brief," he jabbed a finger at me, "you know, I know, the king knows, indeed the whole realm knows, that I was a friend of Mortimer. A member of his secret council, but I was not, I repeat, not, involved in Edward II's murder. In my life, I have been many things but never a perjurer and I have publicly sworn my innocence as regards the death of our present king's father." He paused before continuing, "In April 1334 a clerk, John Prickhare, or Prickarse, as I like to call him, came into this very cathedral and accused me of being party to Edward II's murder. The accusation was a serious one so I purged myself by oath, as well as producing irrefutable evidence that when King Edward was killed, I was abroad on a mission to France."

Orleton sipped from a plain pewter goblet. "Naturally," he continued, "my innocence was established. I was free of guilt but not from the suspicion of it. The present king has dismissed me from the council and I have never escaped from the endless circle of rumours concerning my supposed involvement in Edward II's death."

The bishop stopped once more to gulp from the goblet. "Rhenish wine laced with nutmeg," he explained. "It keeps the chill from my bones." He put the goblet down and continued as if there had been no interruption. "Some of the rumours are quite incredible. You have heard of them?"

I shook my head and Orleton, seizing a quill from a portable writing tray, scrawled a few words on a scrap of parchment.

"Of course, you're familiar with Latin?" he inquired. When I nodded, Orleton handed me the parchment and instructed me to construe the following sentence: *"Regem noli occidere, timere bonum est."*

"'Do not kill the king, it is good to be afraid'?" I translated questioningly.

Orleton nodded with satisfaction and quickly scrawled another message for me to read. The phrase was identical to the one before and I was about to hand it back when Orleton told me to scrutinize it more carefully. I did so and noticed that although the words were identical, Orleton had now moved the comma from the *"timere"* forward to the *"occidere,"* so the translation now became "Do not fear to kill the king, it is a good thing."

The bishop must have gathered from my startled expression that I had discovered the new translation for he grinned mirthlessly and slumped back in his chair, a small parchment-knife balanced carefully between his fingers.

"Rumour has it, Master Beche," he explained, "that I sent the second message to Edward II's gaolers in reply to their request about what they should do with the king. Then when there was an official inquiry into his murder after Mortimer's fall from power, I was supposed to have claimed that the comma had been moved. If it comes after the word *'occidere,'* then it reads as you first translated it, a piece of simple advice. The gaolers were not to kill their prisoner, as I expected that they should be frightened of their great responsibilities."

Orleton tossed the knife on to the table and leaned forward. "The story is a complete fable, Master Clerk. I never sent such a message. I was abroad when the old king died and, even if I had been present, I would never have had the authority to issue such an order. So why do I tell you this fable?" Orleton's voice almost rose to a shout. "Simply to illustrate the lies and popular hysteria which still surround Edward II's death. Do you understand?"

I hastily reassured him that I did. I also realized Orleton could tell me little although his account had flushed one hare from the corn.

"My lord," I began, "you mentioned both the king's gaolers and an official inquiry into the horrible crime they committed. Who were these gaolers and was there really an inquiry?"

For a while Orleton stared hard at the rafters above my head before telling me that Edward II had been imprisoned at Berkeley Castle in Gloucestershire. The king had been under the direct supervision of Sir Thomas Berkeley, father of the present seigneur. Lord Berkeley, he explained, was tried by his peers at the November Parliament of 1330 and declared innocent of any involvement in Edward II's murder.

I pressed Orleton for the reasons for such a verdict, but he claimed his memory was failing. He did admit that there had been other gaolers involved in the murder but these were never brought to trial as they had fled overseas.

Orleton rose wearily as if exhausted by the violence of his speech and extended a gnarled hand for me to kiss, a sign that the audience was over. I was about to withdraw when he suddenly called out, "Master Beche, I do wish you success with your commission." I turned expectantly, for his tone conveyed more than a pleasant dismissal, but the bishop shook his head.

"No," he said softly, "there's little to add, except that it was I who heard Mortimer's last confession. You know canon law, Master Beche, and realize I cannot account for what passed between us but, after I had given absolution, I questioned Mortimer about Edward II's death. It's strange. The fellow swore he had not killed the king. Of course, I tried to press him further but he refused to say any more. I thought it peculiar. Don't you, Master Clerk?"

Naturally, I agreed with him. I thanked him for his assistance, then withdrew, rather confused about some of the details of my conversation with him.

I returned to the inn and packed my saddle-bags for an immediate return to London. I remember little of that journey, neither the clinging cold during the day nor the warmth and food of the inns where I lodged at night. I was totally taken up with what Orleton had told me. His remarks about Mortimer, I quickly dismissed. The dead baron had been the bishop's friend and patron which would account for Orleton's attempt to clear his name. Even if the bishop was correct, Mortimer could have been lying or, more probably, using some legal quibble to clear himself of any personal guilt in Edward II's death. No, what fascinated me, Richard, was Orleton's reference to the official investigation at the November Parliament of 1330. The great rolls of Parliament, preserved in the muniment room of the Tower of London, would have recorded such an event and this fact led me to consider a different approach to my inquiry.

So far, I had relied on personal witness but Orleton had demonstrated the flaws of such a method which relied on hearsay, prejudice, half-truths and even deliberate lies. Moreover, most of the important witnesses were either dead or unapproachable. Consequently, by the time I entered Cripplegate early this afternoon, I had decided that the answers for which I was searching could lie here in London. As you know, Richard, the English may despise good government but they have an almost religious awe for competent administration. Ever since the early days of Henry the Angevin, this administration has revolved around the Chancery and the Exchequer. The former is the royal writing office which issues all writs, letters and proclamations whilst the latter is the treasury, controlling the revenues of the crown. Both are subject to royal scrutiny and so both keep meticulous accounts which they deliver annually to the great muniment room in the Tower. Of course, I am acquainted with both and I decided to reconstruct Edward II's imprisonment by a thorough scrutiny of all government records for the year 1327.

Such records, however, would only provide the facts but no narrative, no contemporary account. When I got back to my lodgings, I lay fully dressed on my bed wondering where I could find such a source. Then the bells of St Paul's Cathedral began to ring out for Saturday vespers. The cathedral dominates Bread Street and the constant tolling of its bells from matins to compline have always irritated me, but this time they came as an answer to a prayer. The cathedral is staffed by canons and I am on cordial terms with their archivist, Simon Islip. I remembered a chance meeting a few months earlier when we discussed the highly delicate task of preserving vellum. Islip was greatly concerned with this matter as he was responsible for the annals of his cathedral which, he proudly maintained, served as a valuable history, not only of the capital but of the country at large. These annals may be the very things I need, a contemporary account of the events surrounding the death of Edward II.

So, dear Richard, without stirring abroad, I can finish this wretched business. Tonight, I shall celebrate with a meal and a romp with my Kate, a description of whose charms and arts would only offend your celibate nature. I bid you adieu. God keep you. Written at Bread Street, 6 November 1345.

Letter Three

Edmund Beche to his friend, Richard Bliton, Prior of Croyland Abbey, greetings.

I closed my last letter, Richard, so confident that my work amongst the records would finally finish the task, but they have simply clouded the matter further. At the same time I wrote to you, I also sent a report to the king, describing my interview with Orleton and explaining what I intended to do. His grace replied promptly. He expressed special interest in the bishop's last meeting with Mortimer and ordered me to report again once he returns from his campaign against the French.

I began my research at St Paul's and in the Tower Muniment Room and, within three weeks, I was able to draw up a fairly accurate picture of Edward II's capture and imprisonment. In 1322, after crushing his barons at the battle of Boroughbridge, Edward II and the Despenser family began to rule England like despots. Despenser the Younger totally controlled the king's decisions and waged a savage vendetta against Isabella, who refused to accept his authority. He confiscated her lands and even organized a plot to allow the Scots to capture her. He insisted on sleeping in the same room as the King and encouraged Edward's affection for his own wife, Eleanor. In 1325, under the pretext of a diplomatic mission to France, Isabella managed to leave England. A few months later she was joined by her eldest son (the present king) and, together with the exiled Roger Mortimer (who had escaped from the Tower), moved to Hainault in the Low Countries where she planned her invasion of England.

Isabella and Mortimer landed in Suffolk in September 1326 with a few followers. Popular discontent at Edward II's rule drew almost everyone to their standards, especially as the queen was shrewd enough to pose as the champion of justice and the avenger of the wrongs committed by the Despensers. When Henry, the new Earl of Lancaster, joined Isabella, this was the signal for a general desertion of her husband's cause. The king soon found himself unable to resist the united opposition centred around the queen; within weeks, even the rats from the administration began to desert him. The very courtiers who had been the chief agents of Despenser, the self-seeking bishops, the corrupt judges and the time-serving royal agents went over almost as a body to the side of Isabella and Mortimer. Edward was in London when his queen landed but the anger of the mob soon drove him out of the city. He tried to make a stand at Gloucester, where he unfurled the royal banner, but no one answered his summons, so he crossed the River Severn to the county of Glamorgan. There he made one more pathetic attempt to maintain a foothold in England. Despenser's father was sent back to hold Bristol but he only attracted the attention of Isabella, who besieged the city. After a few days, Despenser the Elder surrendered. He was shown no mercy but dragged through the city and beheaded.

Meanwhile, Edward was wandering aimlessly through Glamorgan. Isabella, intent upon his capture, despatched some of her faithful followers to track him down. On 16 November 1326, Edward and his pitifully few retainers were betrayed at Neath in South Wales, captured and marched off to the castle of Llantrissant. Hugh Despenser the Younger, however, was taken to the queen at Hereford. There, he was dragged through the city shrieking with terror, before being hanged, quartered and beheaded. Isabella had a banqueting table placed beneath the scaffold so she could eat and drink while she watched her enemy die. As for Edward II, Isabella refused to meet him and ordered him to be imprisoned at Monmouth Castle.

I have now reached my real subject, Richard, the captivity and death of Edward II. After a short time at Monmouth, Edward was escorted to the castle of Kenilworth, where he remained under the care of the Earl of Lancaster. Meanwhile, Isabella and Mortimer consolidated their victory. A parliament met on 7 January at Westminster, where it was decided that Edward should be deposed for incompetence and his son put in his place. A deputation from this parliament visited Kenilworth and offered Edward the alternatives of either resignation or deposition. The poor king showed little fight and was forced to accept the inevitable. He was led in front of the deputation, clad in black, and, dazed with confusion, tearfully announced that he would yield to the wishes of Parliament and appoint his son as his successor. Then the leader of the deputation renounced homage and the steward of the old king's household broke his wand of office to indicate that Edward II's reign was finished.

The pathetic ex-king was then led back to captivity. The records maintain his treatment at Kenilworth was good. He lacked nothing and was honoured as a closely guarded state prisoner. This is quite likely, for although Henry of Lancaster had taken a leading part in bringing about the king's deposition, he was profoundly conscious that his prisoner had been his anointed prince. However, Isabella seems to have thought that Lancaster was too kind. At the beginning of April 1327, Edward was taken from the care of Lancaster and transferred to Berkeley Castle under Lord Thomas Berkeley and a Somerset knight, John Maltravers.

Here, Richard, begins the last stage of Edward II's captivity, and it is hidden in both mystery and tragedy. Once Edward was at Berkeley, the account of the chronicle of St Paul's becomes very meagre and I could only trace the details of the king's imprisonment at Berkeley Castle from the dusty documents now stored in the Tower Muniment Room. I can start with a few known facts. Custody of Edward was vested in Thomas Berkeley and John Maltravers on 3 April 1327 and within a few days of this, an allowance of Five pounds per day was assigned to these two, "for the expense of the household of the Lord Edward, formerly King of England." At first, this seems a generous amount. Five pounds a day could keep many a man in considerable comfort, but whether the money was actually spent on poor Edward seems dubious. The chronicle of St Paul says he was much ill-used and his captors may have regarded the allowance merely as a bribe to abuse their unfortunate prisoner. One rather surprisingly new fact was that Berkeley and Maltravers were assisted by two others, Thomas Guerney and William Ockle. In fact, this precious pair were the actual gaolers, whilst Maltravers and Thomas Berkeley were merely custodians of the castle. Landed gentry might have a healthy respect for a royal prisoner, but the same cannot be true of anonymous killers who would gleefully crucify their mothers.

The garrulous chronicle had other gems in store for me. Once Edward was transferred to Berkeley Castle, rumours began to ciruclate that there was a plot to free him. The ring-leader of this plot was Brother Stephen Dunheved, a Dominican friar, an eloquent preacher and confessor to the deposed king. If the chronicle is to be believed, Edward II had sent this friar to the papal court to secure a divorce from Isabella. On his return from this fruitless quest, Friar Stephen found his former master had been deposed and at once began to plot his release. Fresh urgency was lent to his efforts by the rumours which had begun to circulate concerning Edward's ill-treatment at Berkeley. According to these whispers, the deposed king was kept in a pit along with decaying animal corpses and only his splendid constitution saved him from a pestilential death. By the beginning of July 1327, Dunheved was ready. Men from many different regions and professions banded themselves together to free their former king. According to the chronicle of St Paul, Dunheved launched his attack against Berkeley Castle on the night of 16 July. He managed to enter the castle by stealth but his attempt to free the king failed. The chronicle does not say what happened to either Dunheved or his followers.

It seems that Isabella and Mortimer then decided to murder Edward and despatched the necessary orders to Berkeley Castle. On the night of 21 September 1327, Guerney and Ockle entered the king's cell. They forced him down to the floor and thrust a red-hot iron up into his bowels so as to kill him without leaving any trace of violence on the body. The king's hideous shrieks, however, told the entire castle of his horrible death and drove many to their knees to pray for his soul. After his death, it then appears that from 21 September to 21 October, Edward's corpse remained at Berkeley under the custody of his former gaolers, for which they were paid five pounds per day. Isabella and Mortimer had decided that the dead king should be buried at the nearby cathedral of Gloucester but even when the body was removed from Berkeley, Guerney and Ockle remained responsible for it. They conveyed the royal corpse to the chapter house of Gloucester Cathedral, where it lay in state for a few days before being solemnly interred in the cathedral itself.

Once I had finished a detailed reconstruction of the late king's imprisonment, I immediately became aware of one glaring discrepancy. The chronicle of St Paul, popular opinion and even His Grace the king all categorically maintain that Edward II was murdered on the Feast of St Matthew, 21 September 1327. Yet, according to these same records, all orders for the feeding and housing of the royal prisoner suddenly end on 21 July, some two months before his death.

For a while, every effort on my part to fill this gap in the records proved futile. First, I attempted to explain it through an omission in the records themselves, but this would not account for the total absence of any mention of the imprisoned king. I then considered the possibility of Edward II being starved to death, but this contradicted the theory that he was violently murdered. Moreover, a man starved of all food would not take over eight weeks to die and, if his corpse was displayed to the public view, such emaciation could be sufficient proof that he had been murdered.

I could find no solution and decided upon an immediate visit to Berkeley Castle, despite the snow and sleet of this miserable winter. There, I hoped to find some record of the king's gaolers requisitioning supplies locally, although this was a vague hope from the start. The exchequer had carefully supervised the royal prisoner's welfare since his capture in December 1326 and there was no reason why such care should suddenly end two months before Edward II's death. Nor was there evidence of any order transferring the responsibility for Edward's welfare from London to his gaolers. I, therefore, concluded that a visit to Berkeley was essential. His Grace the King would certainly think me careless if I failed to visit the castle where his father had been imprisoned.

Once I had decided on the journey, I began my preparations. I left London on Saturday, 22 January. I took my mare and a sumpter-pony laden with a change of robes, provisions and blankets. The exchequer had answered my draft for fifty marks, twenty-five of which went into my purse whilst I stitched the rest into my thick leather sword-belt. Kate went with me to Aldgate to bid me an affectionate farewell though I had little doubt she would soon console herself. Once I was out of the city, I travelled north-west through Acton, Ruislip and Wallingford, towards the Berkeley demesne.

The journey was bitterly cold. A leaden grey sky and the countryside, so beautiful in summer, were hidden by driving winds and sleet. I passed through small, squalid hamlets and stayed at a series of miserable inns, where the one topic of conversation was the war against the French and the government's insistent demands for war supplies. The people I met were dressed like scarecrows, scavenging in hedges and fields for anything to eat. Their lot is pitiable. The men are recruited for the king's wars, and only the crippled return, thrown out to fend for themselves. Even in time of peace, whatever the season, the peasants are heavily taxed. In summer, the royal purveyors move like a plague from village to village collecting produce and after them, the tax-collectors, followed by the bailiffs and sergeants of the local seigneurs. Where I could, I distributed some of the money I had received and it was taken without thanks by cold, grasping hands. I had heard about the growing violence in the countryside and now I witnessed it firsthand. On a number of occasions, I passed corpses decomposing in ditches and, at every crossroads, the gibbets were heavy with their rotten human fruit. The intense cold kept me safe, for only once was I threatened, outside Wallingford, by a group of ruffians, who soon dispersed when they heard the hoofbeats of a scouting convoy from Wallingford Castle.

My near escape did not deter me and I pressed on, until a

week after leaving London the battlements of Berkeley Castle appeared on the skyline. The castle, dominating the western road linking the North and Southwest of the country, is situated on a plateau some fifty feet above the floodable meadows of the River Avon. The great keep soars high and on its turret fluttered a multi-coloured banner emblazoned with the arms of the Berkeleys. The morass which surrounds the castle's crenellated walls forced me on to the causeway which led to the main gate. I was about twenty paces from it, when a voice rang out, ordering me to stop and state my business. I tried to raise my voice above the wind, waving the royal commission as if it was a pennant. After a long, silent wait a postern door opened. I dismounted and led in my mare and then returned for the sumpter-pony. The door was slammed behind me and a serjeant clattered down from the parapet, shouting questions at me. I curtly informed him I was on the king's business and wished to speak to Sir Maurice Berkeley. The man nodded and bawled at a shivering groom to look after my nags. He led me across the outer and inner baileys, into the keep and up a flight of stairs to the great hall of the castle.

It was a long spacious room, with black rafters spanning walls covered in silken Flemish tapestries. At the far end, a few figures, huddled in great cloaks, lounged around the high table. My guide bade me stay where I was and hurried forward to an over-dressed young man sitting in the centre of the group. I knew this must be Lord Berkeley. After a brief conversation with the serjeant, Berkeley beckoned me forward and stood to receive the commission I held. Despite his rich robes, Berkeley is no fop; his muscular frame, fiery red hair and tense scarred face mark him as a soldier, more suited to the camp than the court. He scanned my commission, said a few words to his companions and led me over to a window embrasure. The arrow slit was sealed with wooden shutters and we crouched on stools around a small, sweet-smelling brazier. Berkeley came swiftly to the point and asked if I had come to question him, or simply to see the cell where the king's father had died. I told him both, and added that I would like to inspect the accounts for Berkeley Castle during the period Edward II was held prisoner there. Berkeley asked why and I glibly informed him that the king wanted my history to be based on documentary evidence, as well as verbal accounts. He seemed satisfied with this reply and I thought the interview over when he began to speak softly, as if to himself.

"Edward II's death was a crime, Master Clerk. A perpetual stain on the Berkeley name, but the real pity is that my father knew nothing about it. God rest his soul."

"How's that?" I asked.

Berkeley looked intently into the brazier. "Because, Master Clerk, my father was not at Berkeley when the king was killed, but at Bradby, a few miles away, suffering from an illness which nearly proved fatal. Believe me, this is no fable. My father's absence was attested to by many independent witnesses."

I was impressed by the man's earnestness, but equally determined to exploit his eagerness to clear his family's name.

"My lord," I asked tentatively, "did you or your father notice anything peculiar or extraordinary during the late king's imprisonment?"

Berkeley pursed his lips. "You must understand," he replied, "that though Edward II was imprisoned here, the Berkeleys were not responsible for his custody. My father was a kinsman of Mortimer, but he was a sick man and used his illness as an excuse to leave this castle as often as possible. Mortimer chose this place because of its vast remoteness, as well as its proximity to his own lands on the Welsh border. The castle was filled with Mortimer's retainers and Edward II's imprisonment was entrusted to three of Mortimer's closest henchmen, Sir John Maltravers, Sir Thomas Guerney and William Ockle. The first was a Somerset knight who hated the deposed king. Guerney was a professional killer and Ockle was a hunchbacked, misbegotten nonentity." Berkeley paused for a moment. "Maltravers had little to do with the prisoner. He was simply my father's lieutenant and custodian of the castle. He has been accused of being involved in the murder but Guerney and Ockle kept the king even from him. In fact, this precious pair kept themselves and their captive from public view and only spoke to the messengers Mortimer sent from Westminster. No one in the castle even knew that the king had died until it was announced a few days afterwards that he had expired from natural causes, and then Guerney ordered us all to leave the keep while the royal body was prepared for burial in Gloucester Cathedral."

"Were the preparations for burial carried out there?"

"No, here," Berkeley explained, jabbing his finger at the floor, "in the great hall itself, but no one was allowed admittance. Not even the royal clerks who brought the shroud, coffin and other materials for the burial."

"Then who dressed the corpse?"

"Ah, now that's strange. Not any court physician, but an old woman, a witch from the Forest of Dean. She was hired by Queen Isabella to prepare her husband's body for burial and then disappeared."

"So no one saw the corpse?"

Berkeley laughed drily. "For a clerk, you have a fanciful imagination, Master Beche. No, the old woman was probably hired because a skilled physician would soon recognize that the king had died violently. However, we all saw the corpse before its burial. It was taken from here to Gloucester, where it lay in state, its face uncovered for days, before being buried with great pomp in the cathedral."

"Do you know how the King actually died?" I asked.

Berkeley shrugged. "You've heard the stories," he replied. "I've never heard anything different. The King was abused before he died, he had a reputation as a sodomite and Guerney and Ockle were spiteful, twisted bastards."

Even though a great deal of his story tallied with what I had already learnt from the records in the Tower Muniment Room, I thought that Berkeley's narrative contained many valuable items of information. The most important were the reasons for the great secrecy which had surrounded the king's death. Naturally, his assassins would only be too eager to hide any evidence of the crime.

After a moment's reflection, I asked Berkeley why Edward had been so closely guarded. I pointed out that he was far from popular, which accounted for the success of his wife's invasion.

"There were rumours," the man replied, "that some fanatics were plotting to free him. There were reports of groups gathering in the Forest of Dean and all along the Welsh March. Strangers were seen and reported in the surrounding hamlets, many armed contrary to the government's instructions. One group, led by a monk Dunheved, actually attacked the castle and managed to get down to the old king's cell, where they murdered one of the guards, a Gascon called Bernard Pellet. Anyway, most of the attackers were killed or captured before being beaten off. The rest, including Dunheved, got away. I believe he and his band were later rounded up by Mortimer's agents and disappeared for ever." Berkeley paused and smiled wryly, "I remember all these details for I was 16 and all agog with curiosity."

After that, Berkekey began to ask for news from London and the court. He said that he had been serving with the army abroad and was eager to return. When I asked why he had not joined the court in London, he shrugged and explained that he had been at Berkeley since the previous June when the king had visited the castle.

"Did he inspect his father's dungeon?"

Lord Berkeley shook his head. "No, he showed no interest in the place. In fact, he and Sir John Chandos spent most of their time in Gloucester, inspecting the cathedral."

Berkeley then chatted freely about the king's wars before he cut himself short with an apology and offered to show me where the king's father had been imprisoned. I quickly accepted and Berkeley, taking a torch from the wall, led me down the cold, draughty stairwell to the base of the keep. There he began to tug at a ring on one of the damp sandstone flags. After a great deal of effort, he managed to raise it on to its side. In the flickering torchlight, I saw a wooden ladder going down into the darkness. Lord Berkeley, tightly gripping his torch, descended and I followed a little more carefully. The cell was really an underground cave and I saw there were signs that it had once been occupied. Sconces to hold rushlights rusted on the wall and a rotting mass of straw in a far corner probably once served as a bed. Berkeley explained that when the cell was occupied, the ladder was taken up and the flagstone replaced while small slits in the floor above ensured the prisoner did not suffocate. As I inspected this place of abomination, flickering and dancing in the light of the torch, I silently prayed for the king who must have crouched there before dying in unspeakable agony. The place stank of mildew and the sickly sweetness of decay. I felt as if I was in some antechamber of hell and was only too grateful to get out. I courteously declined Lord Berkeley's invitation to dinner and, pleading fatigue, I was shown to a small chamber above the great hall. There, I tried to analyse what I had learnt but my tired brain kept returning to that evil, dark pit until I dropped into a fitful sleep.

The next morning Berkeley showed me the muniment room and the castle account rolls for the years 1326 and 1327. The hour-candles he lit for me had burnt two of their rings before I finished what proved to be a futile search. There was no record of Edward II's being dependent on the supplies of Berkeley Castle after 21 July, 1327. In fact, the records corroborated my findings in London, for there was a roll of receipts which tabled the amounts the Exchequer had sent to Berkeley, as well as their date of issue. The list was identical to the one I had drawn up in London and I noticed with despair that the last sum sent from London was twenty shillings on 21 July, 1327. For a while, I wondered if the present Lord Berkeley could help me solve the mystery. But if his accounts could not help and he was only a lad of 16 when Edward II was murdered, I realized my questions would achieve little except to publicize my secret suspicions.

I left the muniment room and joined Lord Berkeley in the great hall. My disappointment must have been evident but he was too courteous to pry and promised that as soon as I had eaten, his steward, Edmund Novile, would escort me to Gloucester to visit the royal tomb. Novile had been born in the Berkeley demesne and had risen through the domestic ranks to the position of chief steward, a rare achievement for a mere commoner. We left the castle after midday. A watery sun gleamed and glistened on the overnight snow which covered the countryside. As we let our horses amble along the track winding down to Gloucester, Novile forgot his shyness towards a stranger from the great city, and soon became loquacious, a mood I furthered with a mixture of subtle flattery and generous swigs from the wine-skin I carried.

He assured me, his wine-laden breath rising in puffs, that he had been at Berkeley during the late king's imprisonment and was glad when the dreadful business was over. "The castle," he explained, "had crawled with Mortimer's wild Welshmen while Guerney and the little hunchback, Ockle, had ruled like cocks in a barnyard. They had refused everyone entry to the base of the keep and threatened death to anyone who tried to enter it, especially after the Dunheved escapade."

I asked him how that band had managed to penetrate so deeply into the castle, but Novile muttered something about a surprise attack in the dead of night. Somehow, I received the distinct impression that he was sorry Dunheved had failed.

"You know," he added, wiping his mouth after another generous helping from my wine-skin, "that attack was a mysterious affair. I shared a girl with Pellet, the guard who was killed, so I asked Ockle if I could arrange his funeral. The man went pale with fury. He told me to mind my own business as Mortimer had ordered Pellet's body to be kept in spirits for transportation back to his family in Bordeaux."

"Wasn't that rather generous treatment for a Gascon mercenary?"

Novile shrugged. "So I thought. But Guerney said that the Gascon had 'connections.'"

"Was the body sent?"

"I don't know," Novile replied. "Ockle and Guerney increased their vigilance after Dunheved's attack. I don't really know what happened to Pellet's body. Everything was so confused, hidden in a mist of secrecy. But I think it was sent back."

"What happened to the old woman who had been brought in to dress the corpse?" I asked. Novile said he didn't know. He remembered Guerney bringing her to the castle and that was all. She probably disappeared, he added, once she had done her task and been suitably rewarded.

He then lapsed into a filthy diatribe against Mortimer and Isabella, who had brought such dishonour to the Berkeley name. I let him ramble on as I analysed the information both he and his master had given. There were a number of facts I could pursue further. What became of the fighting monk Dunheved and his fellow conspirators? And why was Edward II's corpse dressed by an old woman and not by court physicians?

I was still pondering on these problems when we entered Gloucester. We passed through streets clogged with filthy mush, wary of the snow which cascaded from the sloping roofs. The city, so dependent on the surrounding countryside, was quiet. The streets were deserted except for the occasional, dirty beggar. We slowly made our way to the cathedral, whose magnificent spire must be the pride and glory of the countryside. We left our horses in the cathedral forecourt and walked through the icy slush to the great door. Just as I was about to enter, Novile tugged at my sleeve and pointed back to the middle of the great, empty square.

"There," he exclaimed, "right there! That's where they put the king's corpse."

"Did you see it?"

Novile nodded. "It was laid out in a great coffin, resting on trestles covered with black velvet cloths. The body was dressed in a white shroud and the head covered with a wimple like that of a nun."

"You recognized him as King Edward?"

"Of course," Novile jibed. "His face was shaven but I had seen Edward on the few occasions he had visited Berkeley, before his wife started to play the two-backed beast with Mortimer. Why?" he added abruptly. "Who else could it have been? Don't forget the corpse was also seen by Edward II's family and leading courtiers." I hastened to explain that Mortimer's ruffians could have so ill-treated the king that they might have substituted his corpse with another. Novile laughed outright and, shaking his head with amusement, led me by the arm into the cathedral.

We walked up the main aisle, genuflected to the high altar and turned left towards the decorated tabernacle of Edward II's tomb. It is truly magnificent. On a huge white slab hewn out of pure marble rests a life-like effigy of the murdered king, resplendent in marble robes and crown. Above this is an intricately carved canopy of stone, supported by slim pillars which allow the visitors to view but not touch the beautiful effigy. Novile explained that the tomb was erected by the king's son. As I studied it, I suddenly realized that there was something further amiss. All English kings are buried at Westminster so why had Edward II been buried here? Because he had been deposed? Or simply out of convenience? I remembered the chronicle of St Paul had maintained that no church, except Gloucester, was willing to accept the royal corpse, for fear of offending Mortimer. I put this to Novile, who stoutly denied it. He remembered a monk from Westminster coming to Berkeley to claim the king's corpse, but, on Mortimer's orders, Ockle and Guerney had rejected the request out of hand. Novile also pointed out that Gloucester was a natural choice. The abbot at the time, Thoki, was a relative of Mortimer, the cathedral was near Berkeley, whilst a funeral procession to Westminster might have only provoked riots in favour of a king whose stupid errors had been wiped out by his sudden death. I was impressed by such arguments but I could see Novile was becoming bored and I suggested a quick return to the castle.

The following morning I left Berkeley. I thanked Lord

Berkeley for his hospitality and travelled as quickly as possible back to London. I arrived back safely on Friday evening and decided to spend Saturday and Sunday, not on affairs of state, but in gentle dalliance with Kate. The wench pouted at my absence but quickly forgave me when I took her to purchase a silver gewgaw in Lombard Street.

On Monday I began my research in the library of Westminster Abbey. I did find numerous petitions from the abbey that Edward II be buried there, as well as the expenses of one of the monks, John Jargolio, who had travelled to Berkeley in a vain attempt to secure possession of the royal corpse. He had travelled to Gloucestershire to seek an interview with Mortimer. This had been refused. Instead, he had to content himself with Guerney who curtly instructed him that Queen-Isabella had decided that Gloucester would be the final resting-place for her husband. The report gave nothing else and so I spent the rest of the week delving into more records to draw up a file on Dunheved's attack on Berkeley Castle. Dunheved himself is not mentioned in any official account until 1 August, 1327 when a warrant was issued for the arrest for "divers crimes" of Thomas Dunheved, his brother Stephen, William Aylmer, John Butler, Peter de la Rockle and Thomas de la Haye. Two weeks later Dunheved was arrested in Yorkshire and committed to Pontefract Castle. The rest of his gang were rounded up by the end of September and thrown into the Fleet prison in London. I checked the expense rolls of both Pontefract and Fleet (whose rolls are always sent to the Exchequer as the gaolers claim for the upkeep of their prisoners) and I was surprised to find that by December 1327 neither Dunheved nor any of his companions had been brought to trial as they had all died from a variety of gaol diseases.

So, Richard, I now have an arm-long list of questions which I cannot answer.

Item – why did the expenses for Edward II suddenly end on 21 July?

Item – what happened during the Dunheved attack on Berkeley Castle?

Item – why did the official accounts omit any reference to an attack on Berkeley Castle, but merely accuse Dunheved of "divers crimes"?

Item – why was Dunheved not brought to trial? And, rank though our prisons be, surely it is strange that he and all his collaborators died of gaol fever within three months of their arrest?

Item – why was an old woman and not royal physicians brought to dress the corpse of the dead king?

Item – why were Guerney and Ockle so secretive in their custody of the king?

Item – why did Mortimer categorically refuse to hand over the dead king's body to the Abbey of Westminster?

Item – just how did Edward II die?

Taken individually, I know there is probably a plausible answer to each of these questions, but taken together, they do cast serious doubts on the accepted version of Edward II's murder. Roger Bacon once said that "Truth is the daughter of time." But time waits for no man, Richard, and I have decided to approach the queen dowager Isabella. She may solve all my problems and I think I am well equipped to coax fresh answers from her.

I have decided not to inform the king of my intentions, for I shall merely report that I am investigating the Dunheved conspiracy. I beg you to continue to keep silent. God keep you Richard. Written at Bread Street, 22 February, 1346.

Letter Four

Richard Bliton to Edmund Beche – greetings, I have decided to ignore your advice and, on this occasion at least, reply to you. It was good to receive your letter. It is a pity that such mysterious circumstances have prompted it, but I am sure His Grace the King knows what he is doing. Must you show disrespect both to him and our lord archbishop? Should you be breaking their confidence? I would liked to have been consulted first. I do hold an important position in the Church which cannot be compromised. However, I have given the matter careful thought and believe my rank and status make me the best possible confidant. I would have liked to reply earlier but I had to travel to London on urgent priory business. My real purpose in writing is to warn you not to be impulsive. The king may think you are a steady, industrious clerk but I know you to be stubborn, impetuous and proud. I warn you to be careful and confide in me.

My second reason for writing was to impart certain information. As you know, Croyland has its own chronicle, and I have spent two busy days of my precious time in researching on your behalf. There are the usual entries about Isabella's invasion and rule, but the following entries may be of use to you. The first is a confession and I give it to you verbatim:

In the name of the Father, the Son and the Holy Ghost, I, Brother Thomas Marshall, took this confession from John Spilsby, master carpenter, at his behest on 14 March, 1332.

My name is Spilsby. I was born in Grantham and became an apprentice carpenter. My skills, thank God, gave me preferment and I entered the service of the crown as a Master Craftsman. A position I held till an accident crushed my legs and brought me a king's pension to die at Croyland. My life was an uneventful yet quietly fulfilled one. I worked on wood and loved the craft I followed. Life, politics, even religion passed me by. This ended in the winter of 1327. Like everyone at court I knew that the old king had been overthrown and imprisoned at Berkeley Castle. I was working in Gloucester Cathedral at the time, aware of what had happened but not really bothering. That is until the summons came. It was from the old queen. I was ordered to Berkeley Castle on a secret and private matter. I knew that Edward II had died and I guessed with dread, why I had been summoned. I was taken to Berkeley by a large, uncouth Scottish mercenary and given lodgings in the castle. A room in the keep, small, sparse but clean. There were none of Berkeley retainers. I understood that these had been cleared out and the place was garrisoned by Mortimer's wild Welsh. Except for the keep and the main hall, these were under the direct command of the group I later learnt were the regicides, the old king's gaolers, Guerney, Maltravers and Ockle. For days I kept in my room, food, drink and a change of clothing and bedding were regularly supplied. Eventually, Guerney came to see me. Tricked out in gorgeous colours, he reminded me of a weasel I had once seen; sleek, pampered, well fed and dangerous. He was curt. I was there to measure up the late king's body for a state coffin to be placed in the cathedral. My protests were ignored. A bag of gold was thrust in my hand and I was told to be ready that evening.

I waited all day and thought that Guerney had forgotten me when I heard a rap on my door and Guerney's hoarse whisper of a summons. I threw my cloak round me and opened my door, Guerney and a misshapen hunchback, I later learned to be Ockle, were waiting for me. They held torches, I always remember those torches, the way they flickered, spluttered and revealed the gargoyle features of the regicides. I was taken down to the main hall of the castle. It was cold and deserted. A poor light was given by a few ensconced rushlights which lit up the long trestle table on the dais at the top of the hall. As we approached it, I began to shiver. I had seen Edward II in life. I had never thought that I would be the one to measure his corpse. I found I could not stop the panic within me. The hall was so quiet, so cold and dominated by the corpse lying huddled under a thick purple robe. I turned to Guerney and asked:

"The king?"

Guerney stopped and turned, his eyes as cold and black as any marble.

"The former king," he rasped.

We then walked to the dais. Guerney told me not to lift the cloak but simply measure the corpse. He would stand by me. I recognized the threat, knew he was armed and was more than aware that, though the hall was deserted, it was surrounded by every cut-throat in Wales. I shrugged my shoulders. It was a job. I was not responsible for that terrible figure lying so quietly under the cloth. I started my work, the measuring rod clutched in my hand as tightly as a vice. My task was nearly completed, I measured the body and made a few notes which Guerney carefully checked. Then it happened. Perhaps it was the poor light, or my own fears, but, as I moved to the top of the table, I stumbled and collided with Guerney. For a second we stood poised, then both of us crashed against the table. It quivered, then gently, almost gratefully, it let its terrible burden slide from under the purple cloth on to the floor. I watched in terror. In the poor light I saw a shaven blond head, a pale face and legs, and, as the body rolled in its white shroud, I saw the blue-black holes of the stab wounds. Then everything went black as Guerney threw a cloak over my head. His arm wrapped round my neck like an iron collar, and I felt the prick of a dagger against my heart.

"That was a mistake, Master Mason," he whispered. "An unfortunate accident. You saw nothing."

I nodded, terrified at what I had seen and that piece of steel so near to my heart. Guerney pushed me off the dais, removed the cloak and hustled me out of the hall to where Ockle was waiting. The hunchback must have heard the crash, for he began to babble with questions. Guerney silenced him with an order to take me back to my room and, as we left, I heard the hall doors close behind us. That night I expected to die, I could not sleep for fear for my own safety and at what I had seen. Nothing happened. The next morning Guerney came to my chamber and handed over to me the illegible notes I had made the night before. He did not refer to the events of the previous night except to stare at me before saying that I would be taken back to Gloucester that same day. I realized then that the only reason I was being left unharmed was that Guerney wished to protect himself.

That afternoon, the same Scottish bully took me back to Gloucester. I was excused from normal work and, when the timber arrived, began work on the coffin. Within a week it was finished and sent by road to Berkeley. I received a fresh purse of gold and to all intents and purposes my task was finished. Nevertheless I could not forget that whirling white body, the lolling head the blue-black mouths of the wound. I saw it roll towards me in my dreams. I knew I had seen the body of the murdered king. But whom could I tell? Who would want to know? Who would care? I went to be shriven but my tongue refused to describe what my eyes had seen. Then the accident occurred. A timber slipped and I was thrown into space and blackness. I remembered opening my eyes after I fell only to feel the savage pain in my legs and back. I thought I saw Guerney's face in the crowd which surrounded me, but that must have been a delusion. I was discharged from the king's service and sent to Croyland Abbey. Now, I am dying, I can tell everything and get rid of the haunting vision of a whirling white body with its blue-black gems.

The confession, cryptic as it is, then ends. Spilsby died a few days later and Brother Thomas too is dead. All that is left is this confession of a broken man. You may use this information for its worth. The second piece of information is more mysterious. Whilst searching among the chronicle entries I came across the following:

In the year 1328, royal commissioners, Sir Robert Brabazoun and Sir John Eyatt came to the abbey bearing the commission of the Queen Isabella and Roger Mortimer, Earl of March. They did not reveal the reason for their visit, though we were given to understand that similar visits were made to other monasteries. They brought soldiers from the retinue of Lord Mortimer, who searched the monastery and all its outbuildings. A survey was also made of all in the abbey and then the commissioners left. They did, however, tell the Lord Abbot that official searchers would be appointed to watch the coast, and they would be based in the abbey. Then they left.

I never found out the reason for their visit, and the searchers stayed in the abbey until Mortimer fell. I once met Sir Robert Brabazoun, it was after Isabella's fall from power, and I asked him about his visit. He just smiled and said that he was no wiser. He, like the other commissioners, had been told by Mortimer that they would know what they were looking for when they found it.

So elliptical! I hope this letter has been of use to you, Edmund. Remember my advice about the king and confide in me if you must, but do remember my position. God keep you. Written at Croyland – February 1346.

Letter Five

Edmund Beche to Richard Bliton – greetings. I am sending this letter in haste, so I apologize for the scrawled handwriting and the inferior parchment. I received your letter with some surprise, as I did not expect or ask for a reply. Of course, I will always remember your position, as if I would be allowed to forget it. Nevertheless, it was good of you to write and send the information you did. I do not know what to make of Spilsby's last confession. Did the murderers of Edward II really expect that the people believed the old king had just died in prison? Spilsby's confession tells me little new. Regarding the searches made at Croyland, I cannot comment though I understand such searches are quite common in times of crisis.

What really concerns me is Spilsby's implicit admission that his involvement in the affair at Berkeley led to his maiming. I can understand his fears. I, too, share them. What do you know of Sir John Chandos? The question is a rhetorical one. It is just that the man mystifies and, indeed, frightens me. Two days after the despatch of my last letter, I arrived back at my lodgings. A grandiose description for a room above a merchant's warehouse. As I mounted the winding wooden stairs I noticed that the door of my small room was slightly ajar. At first, I thought it was the work of some of London's riff-raff. Nothing is safe nowadays and burglary and housebreaking are almost as popular as drunkenness. I drew the small dagger I always carried and with forced bravado pushed open the door. Nothing was disturbed, no disarray except for Chandos, who was lying on my rough truckle bed staring at the ceiling, almost parodying the way I do. He never moved as I came in but kept staring upwards. I slumped on to the only stool in the room and waited, quite determined not to show my nervousness at what was an unwarrantable intrusion. At last he turned his head towards me.

"Good-day, Master Clerk. You've kept me waiting."

I tried to hide my annoyance in the sarcastic rejoinder that I did not know that he was coming, and I could not remember inviting him. Chandos smiled and swung his legs off the bed to sit, head in hands, on the edge. He looked tired and travel-stained but his face still had that predatory cruel look.

"How is your research?" he asked bluntly.

I repeated verbatim the report that I had sent to the king. He seemed to listen for a while, but then interrupted me.

"Don't you find it strange to be involved in such a task?"

"No," I lied. "His Grace's father died, was murdered in mysterious circumstances, and this mystery must be clarified."

"You find nothing strange?" The same question in a different way.

"Well," I said, "apart from the fact that the money supply to Berkeley ended two months before Edward II's death."

Chandos shrugged. "There's little mystery there," he pointed out. "We understand that Guerney paid for food from his own purse, hoping to reclaim it later."

I knew this was a lie. I am a trained clerk and I had been through the necessary issues. There had been no such payments to Guerney. However, I nodded as if fully satisfied on that part.

"Anything else?"

The question was so abrupt and so apparently harmless, yet I found it difficult to control my mounting panic. I realized that Chandos might suspect there was and I decided that further protestations on my part would make matters worse.

"There was the question of the Dunheved attack."

"What about it?" he replied.

I hastened to list my queries about how they had been able to penetrate Berkeley Castle and the fact that, despite all of the gang being captured, none had been brought to trial. Chandos seemed unperturbed. He pointed out that that attack had been launched at night, they had received help from within the castle, and they had got no further than the outer bailey. He added that when the Dunheved gang was arrested they had been wounded, exhausted and too weak to withstand the ravages of gaol fever.

"It's a terrible disease, Master Clerk," he concluded, looking straight at me. "It would be a terrible way to die."

The quiet, implied threat stung me into a question I had thought about but never intended to ask.

"Sir John, you seem well informed regarding the details of Edward II's death. Why hasn't the king commissioned you to do this assignment?" He shrugged, his eyes slid from my face to a point above my head.

"I read your reports to the king, and I know something of what happened." He paused. "Anyway, I am not a clerk, and His Grace the King seems pleased with what you are doing."

Before I could acknowledge the compliment, Chandos brusquely passed on to ask, "You are keeping the matter confidential?"

"Of course." The lie tripped off my tongue so quickly that I almost believed it myself.

Chandos then got up and stretched himself. I thought he was going to leave but, as soon as he had wrapped his cloak around himself, he gestured me to follow him and left my room, not even bothering to see if I followed. Of course I did. As we entered the street, I caught up with his long-legged stride and asked where we were going.

"Patience, Master Beche," he replied, "all will be revealed."

I realized I had little option but to follow his advice, quite aware of his two armed retainers, who had detached themselves from a nearby alley to ensure that I did.

I thought wherever Sir John intended us to go, that we would travel by barge, but Sir John turned into Fleet Street to make our way through the bustle and throng of the London crowd. I was too nervous to see where we were going. All I remember is Sir John clearing a path before us as we passed up beyond the writing offices of the Chancery, across the Holborn brook up towards the north-west city gate. It is strange what little pictures remain. There was a friar preaching to an old man and a dog near Holborn Bridge. A whore in a black wig and a scarlet, dirty robe trying to wheedle cash and custom from a well-dressed pimply youth, while behind her a yellow-fanged dog urinated on a drunken cripple. I remember the noise was deafening; hucksters bawling their prices, and children running everywhere, dodging the heavy carts going to and from the river. A Jew stopped counting silver to look at Sir John, before glancing pitifully at me. With his yellow star and hunted look, I was grateful at least for his compassion. Sir John pushed ahead, hardly bothering to turn to see if I followed, fully confident in the two shadows trailing behind me.

Eventually, we turned into the highway which led to the north-west gate of the city. The crowds were thick there and

I wondered why, till I also realized that this road led to the Elms, the favourite execution place for traitors. The crowds were waiting for something. There was an air of tension, even the swarm of itinerant tradesmen looked subdued as everybody craned their necks to where a troop of archers in royal livery kept the road open. Sir John pushed his way through, knocking aside women, children and the occasional bold whore or pickpocket, as if they were merely troublesome flies. I and his two shadows followed in his wake. Eventually, Sir John reached the line of archers and, after a few words, we were allowed through on to the hard, rock-strewn road. Sir John then turned right, and up beyond him I saw the massive T-shaped gallows, ladders and rope black against the sky. I began to shiver, and the stares of the crowd made me think wildly about whether I was going to my own execution. We stopped at the enclosure before the gallows and I stared at the raised platform, the long red-stained bench and black-hooded figures warming themselves around the three glowing braziers. My heart was beginning to pound so violently that I found it difficult to breathe and, when the crowd roared behind me, my panic spilled over. I grabbed Sir John's shoulder, forcing him to turn and look at me. He smiled as if enjoying some secret joke, then quietly removed my sweaty hand from him.

"Don't alarm yourself, Beche," he said soothingly. "It's not for you – is it? Just watch!"

I looked around and saw my two shadows smirking to themselves. My panic and fear subsided. I tried to control my breathing as Sir John led us to the side, to where a group of archers guarded the steps up to the gallows platform. I dimly realized why I was there. I was going to witness an execution. Not mine, but one intended for my benefit. I looked down the avenue where the crowds had roared and I saw a small procession advancing towards us. A number of horses moving slowly, something bumping behind them on the ground, though most of it was masked by its leader, a mounted sergeant and two archers walking beside him. I knew what was coming. I had never witnessed an execution, but I had heard enough to know what terrible bundles those horses pulled. Roger Mortimer had suffered a similar fate, being dragged on a hurdle to these very gallows and then hanged, drawn and quartered. The cavalcade reached us and stopped. I was conscious of men scurrying about, horses whinnying at the smell of blood, shouted orders and the moans of the prisoners. There were two of them, naked except for a loincloth. One quite old with balding pate, wispy beard and thin emaciated body. He had been dragged on a rough sledge from the Fleet prison. He was covered in dirt and his back was one open sore. He seemed only half conscious and two of his guards had to hold him up. His companion was much younger and may have been his son. He may have been quite good-looking but his body was a mass of bloody, muddy gouges. His dark hair and beard were matted with blood. Two dark bruises had half closed his eyes, his mouth was cut and his lower jaw was broken. I will never forget them, not just their wounds – I have seen many before – but the air of restrained terror which surrounded them.

They were hustled past me up on to the platform beneath the gallows. A richly dressed man in robes and chain of office came to the edge of the platform and began to shout from a short roll of parchment. His voice was deadened by the clamour of the crowd which had followed the macabre procession, and now surged like an angry sea around the execution area. Sir John Chandos turned to me and, looking directly into my eyes, said cryptically:

"Traitors, Master Beche. Father and son, they are, well,

were, mariners, who were selling the French information about our navy."

I looked away from him at the grey smoke curling up the braziers, dark against a leaden sky. I tried to look anywhere except at that black platform. The swinging rope, the dancing feet, the roar and animal smell of the crowd. I knew why I was there. I was being taught a lesson, given a warning. I had had enough. I turned and began to push my way through the crowd. I did not care for Chandos or his retainers. It did not matter, they made no attempt to stop me. I stumbled to the edge of the crowd, retched violently and then ran, leaving Chandos, the burning braziers, and those two bodies twisting and dancing. Eventually, I reached Bread Street and the dirty but welcoming warmth of a tavern. I sat there till Kate joined me. I listened to her chatter and drank and thought about the day's events. Why had Chandos gone to such lengths to warn me? What was the real purpose of this assignment? Should I have accepted it? Perhaps, Richard, I should never have written to you, but now we are committed. Written at Bread Street March 1346.

Letter Six

Edmund Beche to Richard Bliton, greetings. It is more than two months since you have heard from me and so much has happened. Then, apart from Chandos's threat, I thought the death of King Edward II was an academic problem. Now it is a mystery which threatens my very existence, as this letter will describe.

After the incident at the Elms I wanted to leave London and I decided it was time to approach the queen mother. I cast about amongst my colleagues and other minor officials of the court as to where the old bitch had gone to earth. Eventually, I discovered the king had ordered her to live in splendid isolation in the great Norman fortress of Castle Rising in Norfolk. I thought it wise not to tell the she-wolf I was coming to her lair, so I packed my belongings and set off for Cambridge. I by-passed that place and, after a week's travel, arrived at King's Lynn. I lodged at The Sea Barque, a bustling tavern where sailors and fishermen from the port of Hunstanton rub shoulders with the burgesses, merchants and farmers of the fertile Norfolk broads. From the inquiries I had made amongst curious locals, I knew that Castle Rising lay a few miles to the east, but I decided to stay in King's Lynn to sniff out the lie of the land before proceeding any further.

I kept to myself, drinking and eating alone, until I merged

with my surroundings. In Norfolk, strangers who bustle in are usually cold-shouldered or, as a local proverb so aptly puts it, "the man who tries to move too fast, never moves at all." I soon became accepted for what I pretended to be, a clerk from Cambridge in pursuit of new employment in some great merchant's house. One evening I managed to draw a group of local farmers into conversation about the queen mother. After some perfunctory remarks about having such a great lady in the area, one of them slammed the table and launched into a surprisingly savage attack upon the old queen. He damned her as a public nuisance, who ruled the area worse than any bishop.

"The old she-wolf," he declared, "rides through the countryside with her bodyguard, taking what she wants. The poor unfortunate she plunders is simply told to present his bills to the sheriff for payment. Of course, the sheriff refers him to London, and who could afford to make such a long trip on the slender hope that the exchequer would make a just and prompt reimbursement?" His words won growls of approval from his companions, but I was more intrigued by the mention of the bodyguard and asked if they were the king's men.

The farmer laughed out loud and dug his red bulbous nose back into his tankard, before explaining. "Master Clerk, they're not king's men but a band of ruffians, hired by the old hag herself and led by some rogue called Michael the Scot."

"Why does the old queen need such protection?" I persisted. "Does she fear attack?"

The farmer shrugged his shoulders. "Perhaps she's frightened of the ghost of her murdered husband. I don't know." He then grumbled on about great lords and ladies and the conversation drifted on to more mundane matters. I sat and let the talk flow on, realizing that the queen I was going to visit had certainly not resigned herself to a gentle retirement. She would have to be approached with great care. I had studied the queen's reputation. Her shrewdness was legendary. In 1313 on a visit to France she met her three sisters-in-law and gave each of them presents of satin gloves. A year later, on a return visit to France, she noticed those same gloves being worn by three young knights of her father's court. Isabella reported the matter to her father, and so initiated a court scandal which rocked France and delighted the rest of Europe. Evidently, Philip's three daughters-in-law had set up a love-nest with these young knights in the Tour de Nesle in Paris, where they met for secret parties and orgies. Their stupid mistake in passing on Isabella's gifts led to their discovery and humiliation. The princesses were immured for life, but their lovers were broken on the wheel at Montfancon. Isabella was dangerous.

The next morning I rose early, dressed carefully and rode out of King's Lynn towards Castle Rising. I reached it about midday, but by-passed the small village and began to make my way up the winding path to the main castle gate. I was about half-way there when a troop of horses emerged from the trees on either side of the track to block my path. I have never seen more fitting candidates for the gallows. They were dressed in a motley collection of gaudy rags but they looked seasoned fighters and were armed to the teeth with swords, daggers, shields and crossbows. Their leader was a huge, beetle-browed man, dressed in half-armour, his head capped in a steel conical helmet, while lying across his saddle pommel was a huge double-edged axe. He cantered towards me and asked my business in a thick, Scots burr which declared, without any introduction, that this was Michael the Scot. I tried to hide my anxiety by curtly informing him that I was on the king's business and wanted an audience

with the queen mother. He asked to see my commission. I
waved it at him but refused to hand it over. He seemed
amused by the gesture for his great, black ugly face broke
into a sneer which ended abruptly as he plucked the reins
from my hand. "If you wish to see the queen, little man," he
roared, "then see her you shall."

Whereupon the rest of the band surrounded us and we set
off at a breakneck gallop up the winding track and
thundered across a drawbridge into the main castle
forecourt. I was dragged from my horse, while deft hands
plucked both my sword and the king's commission from my
grasp, and I was hustled across the yard and up countless
steps into the castle solar. A huge, gaunt room, it dwarfed
the small figure dressed in black who sat near a window
embroidering a piece of tapestry. I was pushed forward and
then roughly forced to my knees as the figure rose and
advanced towards me.

"Eh, Michel," a soft voice asked, *"qu'ce que ce petit homme?"*

"A clerk, your grace," the huge ruffian replied, ignoring
the Norman French. "He carries a royal commission and
claims to be on the king's business."

"Have you the commission?"

"Yes, Your Grace."

"Then we must receive him accordingly. Michael, a chair
for our guest."

I rose and sat. I tried to hide my trembling breathlessness,
my eyes riveted on the queen. Men have called her many
names, "La Belle," "French whore," "Jezebel," "She-wolf,"
yet all I saw was an ageing but still beautiful woman. She sat
opposite me, with Michael the Scot standing beside her, his
helmet in the crook of his arm and his small pig-eyes glaring
at me. I dismissed him with a swift glance of contempt
intended to hide my fear of him and then I turned back to
Isabella. She was dressed in widow-weeds but they were

costly velvet, not sackcloth. Concession had been made to fashion and the long black dress was fringed with Bruges lace around the neck and cuffs, and a silver filigree chain belt clasped her slender waist. Her hair was covered with a black coif but this only enhanced the white, bejewelled fingers which constantly rearranged it with fluttering touches. The face so many men have talked about is heart-shaped, scarcely wrinkled, although slightly marred by pursed lips and violet eyes which never smile.

I must have been gawking like a rustic, for the queen suddenly leaned forward. "Master Beche," she said, "what did you expect? A witch, a crone, a hag?"

She had read my thoughts, but I had the wit to reply, "No Madam, I expected to find a beautiful woman and I am not disappointed. May I thank you for receiving me so courteously."

She caught the drift of my words and smiled. "I am afraid that Michael is over-protective. I found him years ago after," she paused, "after my retirement from state affairs. I took him into my household and he has repaid me with almost fanatical devotion. Anyway," she exclaimed, "enough. How is the court?"

I tried to supply her with all the latest gossip I knew, but I realized it was only to give her time to appraise me. As I spoke, she scrutinized me carefully, and then abruptly interrupted to ask why I had come.

I told her that I was writing a history of her late husband's reign and needed information about his deposition and death. I expected some emotional outburst but instead she was frank and moved swiftly to the point, as if repeating some lesson she had learnt by rote.

"Master Beche," she exclaimed, "I deposed my husband because I hated him, but I took no part in his murder. Mortimer ordered that. I only learnt about it later and I know no more than you or anybody else. I have told the king this many, many times and I cannot understand why he does not follow the words of the Gospel and leave the dead to bury the dead."

"Madam," I tactfully replied, "my real purpose in coming here was not to reopen old wounds, but to seek the answer to several puzzling questions. First, why did the money supplied to your husband suddenly end on 21 July, two months before his death? Secondly, what did happen during Thomas Dunheved's attack on Berkeley Castle in August 1327? Thirdly, why were all of Dunheved's men thrown into jail where they suddenly died before trial? And why was Edward of Caernarvon buried at Gloucester and not in Westminster, among his ancestors?"

I paused for effect before adding, "Finally, madam, what prompted you to hire an old woman to prepare your husband's body for burial when there were skilled court physicians at your beck and call? Who was this woman and where did she go?"

I knew my questions were insolent, but secure in my knowledge of the king's protection, I was also aware that the queen could have played a cat-and-mouse game until the second coming. My bluntness served its purpose. The old vixen was visibly shaken. Her face blanched, her carmine-painted lips opened and shut like a landed fish and she could only regain her composure by lowering her head to examine a be-ringed finger.

"Your questions, Master Clerk, are both abrupt and impertinent," she snapped. "But I shall ignore your rudeness for you will find that there is little profit in it. I can only answer your two final questions, as I am ignorant of the facts behind the rest. Mortimer supervised the king's imprisonment and it was his men who beat off Dunheved's attack and tracked down the rest of the band." The queen then raised her head and smiled deprecatingly as if to imply these matters were now closed, before continuing.

"As to my husband's burial in Gloucester. Well," she shrugged as if the matter was of little concern, "the cathedral was close by, while Westminster was too far away." The queen paused again as if to rearrange her dress, though I noticed her palms were damp with sweat. "The old woman," she continued rather hurriedly, "was hired because I realized that Mortimer had murdered the king. A court physician would have only proclaimed it to the world, and the realm was far too disturbed to accept such a scandal. Who the old woman was and where she went, I cannot tell you because I do not know myself. Anyway, all this happened so long ago. You do understand, Master Beche?"

I understood, but I did not accept her plea of injured innocence. She had been Mortimer's whore and must have loved him. Why else would she have tolerated him for another three years after her husband's murder? In fact, common gossip has it that the night Mortimer was arrested, he was busy tumbling her, and when he was dragged away she was so distraught with grief that she screamed herself into hysterics. Moreover, the queen had been too glib. She maintained that Mortimer's men had taken care of Dunheved, but I had seen the writ confining him to Pontefract and it had been signed and sealed by Isabella herself.

Nevertheless, at the time, I gave every impression that I was satisfied with her explanations. I was beginning to think of suitable phrases to cover a swift withdrawal, when the queen mother suddenly handed me a golden casket from the table beside her and asked me to examine the contents. I opened it and beneath a glass covering lay a human heart, slightly shrivelled, but still well-preserved.

"That," Isabella quietly remarked, "is the heart of my

husband and that is the main reason why I hired the old woman. If a court physician had removed it, Mortimer would have heard about it and been furious. You see, Master Clerk, once Edward was dead, my resentment against him also died. I remembered the golden years of our marriage and wanted his heart to be near me always."

I confess that I was not shocked by the queen's revelation, as I knew that the embalming of a corpse is common amongst the nobility. However, I was surprised that such an act had not been recorded. As I examined the heart of Edward II, I thought of Theobald de Tois. Do you remember him, Richard? He was a skilled physician who lived in Magpie Row at Oxford. We were the only ones who could tolerate him and he thanked us by regaling us with his medical knowledge. He constantly insisted that embalming was a mystery from the East to be practised only by the skilled. So what could an old woman from the Forest of Dean know about such an art? I studied the casket, gathered my wits and then put this to the queen in as disinterested a way as possible. She seemed a little taken aback but said that if I wanted the precise details, then I should have them. The old woman did not embalm the body, she had simply cut through the flesh, broken the ribs and removed the heart, tidying up the cuts and incisions with herbs and plaster. The queen claimed she remembered all this for she insisted that the corpse should show no sign of ill-use, so frightened was she of the possible consequences. She seemed intrigued by my knowledge of medicine and questioned me further, until I was reduced to a few, mumbling phrases.

Isabella hardly noticed. She seemed to have forgotten I was there. She just sat, straight-backed, her hands were tightly clenched and her eyes were staring fixedly past me as if she was looking at long-dead dreams.

"Your visit, Master Clerk," she said in a half-whisper,

"brings back ghosts. Edward of Kent and, above all, gentle Mortimer. A true knight, Master Clerk, but they dragged him, Master Clerk, dragged him by the heels through the filth of London. They hanged and quartered his lovely body, plucked out his heart and left it for the vermin." She turned her fixed gaze on me. "You bring back nightmares, Master Beche. For the last time, leave the dead alone. I cannot and will not speak of these matters again."

Our interview ended, Richard, with me voluble in my thanks and insistence that I could not accept her offer to stay the night in her fortress as my presence was urgently needed in London. The queen nodded understandingly. I kissed her hand and was shown out by Michael the Scot. In the courtyard, he returned both my sword and commission. As I mounted, he pricked my horse in its haunches to send it thundering across the lowered drawbridge to the jeers of the watching garrison. Eventually, the cob broke its gallop whilst my fury at such a graceless exit was outweighed by the relief of getting away unharmed.

Late winter darkness had now shrouded the narrow track, so I let my cob pick its own way down to the village. I could find no inn there but a green bush over a cottage door meant there was a tavern, and for a few coins, I managed to buy sleeping space on the vermin-ridden floor. I drank some of the wine I carried to warm my body as well as soothe my troubled mind, for Queen Isabella was clearly alarmed at my questions, yet she had spoken so smoothly as if what she knew and told me would go no further. But then she had let me go. I was still trying to find the solution to this when I fell into a fitful sleep.

I woke early next morning and, after breaking my fast on a slice of fatty bacon and a tankard of ale, I began my journey back to King's Lynn. The weather made me forget the problems of the previous day. A hoar-frost had hardened the ground and a thick sea mist had swirled in over the countryside. A few miles out of Castle Rising, I found myself on a small track which, I remembered, would lead me down to the crossroads and the road to King's Lynn. Dense forest ran along either side of it and, although the misty silence oppressed me, I only became alarmed when it was suddenly broken by the clink of chained mail. I loosened the sword in my scabbard and then swiftly drew it as a file of hooded figures rose out of the mist to block my way. They were armed with swords and spears and were evidently waiting for me to stop or dismount. I did neither but forced my horse from a trot into a swift gallop and bore down on them, yelling curses and waving my sword, like a veteran of a hundred successful charges. Surprised, they stood disconcerted until I was among them, hacking blindly with terror. I felt my sword cut and bite. A man screamed in agony, another reeled away, his face a bloody mask, and, suddenly, apart from a blow on the cantle of my saddle, I was through them and riding like the wind.

Eventually, I pulled off the track, stopped and, after listening vainly for sounds of pursuit, vomited my breakfast and finally paused to regain some composure. I realized that the ambush was no mere outlaw sortie. If it had been, I would have never known about it until the first shower of arrows. My attackers had been confident that my natural timidity would force a meek surrender, but my sudden charge and the thick concealing mist had foiled their ambush. The attackers could have only been Isabella's men. The queen must have realized that I was aware of her lies. She probably wanted the sources for the questions I had asked, followed by my prompt disappearance into some marsh or unmarked forest grave. The thought of such a quick and violent end only increased my desperation to escape.

I had planned to return to King's Lynn for my sumpter-pony and saddlebags, but I immediately decided to leave Norfolk as quickly as possible. I turned and travelled southeast, the direction my pursuers would least expect me to take. Four days later, I safely reached the port of Harwich and lodged at a dingy, waterside tavern, where I hoped to negotiate a passage for myself and my horse to one of the London ports.

Whilst staying there, I took stock of the situation and, as you may appreciate, Richard, I quickly reached the conclusion that the accepted story of Edward II's murder at Berkeley Castle seemed to be permeated with lies. At first, this had been only a suspicion, but the queen's glib responses and her attempt to kill me, only strengthened the case for further investigation. Yet, if the accepted story was to be discounted, how and with what could I replace it? The records had been exhausted and who else could help me? On my first night in Harwich I sat for hours listening to the sounds of the tavern as I tried to answer these questions. Finally, I drew up a list of all those who knew what had happened during Edward II's imprisonment. I was forced to reduce it to a definite six. Edward himself, Mortimer, Guerney, Maltravers, Ogle and Isabella. But the latter was now unapproachable and the first two were dead, so that left the three murderers. According to the chronicle of St Paul, they had fled to the Low Countries, and then deeper into Germany. Only God knows what forsaken corner of the world shelters them, but finding at least one of them was my only hope. Sir Maurice Berkeley had remarked that Maltravers and Guerney were from Somerset, so I decided I would start there. I dropped all plans to return to London and began to negotiate a passage to one of the Somerset ports.

After a fruitless week's search, I eventually compounded

with a master of a cog, going only as far as Poole, in the shire of Dorset. The king's war with France, so the master pointed out, had led to enemy raids, not only against English shipping in the Narrow Seas, but all along the south coast. Consequently, there had been a sharp reduction in sea-traffic and I should think myself lucky to find a passage at all. The cog, *The Christopher,* was a sturdy craft, owned by a company of merchants, who used it to bring wool from the Yorkshire dales to the south coast, before exporting it to the Low Countries. It had called at Harwich for fresh supplies and, within three days of paying my fee, *The Christopher* was scudding south under a brisk northwesterly.

I was a little seasick at first, but soon I forgot it for once we sighted Dover, the entire atmosphere of the ship changed. The master constantly paced the poop, look-outs were doubled, and the ship's armament prepared in case of attack by the French. Once we were past Dover, the crew relaxed a little as the master brought his ship closer into shore, ready to bolt for harbour should an enemy ship be sighted. I joined the rest of the crew in carrying out their daily tasks, so at night I was too exhausted to think about my own problems. Four days after passing through the Dover Straits, we entered the Solent and the following evening sailed under Crawford Cliffs and into Poole Harbour.

The master helped me disembark my horse and gear. I paid him an extra half mark as a bonus and bade him farewell. For safety's sake, I decided to join a military convoy for the journey inland and so safely reached the town of Dorchester. I stayed there for two days, resting and drawing up a report to the king. Naturally, it differs greatly from what I am telling you. I only informed him of the mystery surrounding the Dunheved conspiracy, Mortimer's refusal to hand Edward II's body over to Westminster and the fact that the queen possessed the heart of the dead king.

I did not mention my growing disbelief of the entire account of his father's death, nor how close I had come to my own outside Castle Rising. I concluded by informing him of my intended visit to Somerset to learn something about the whereabouts of Guerney and Maltravers. I pointed out that I could discover nothing about them in the records and so hoped that there were rumours about their movements in their own native county. I couched the letter in as an obsequious fashion as possible to make them think I had taken Chandos's warning to heart.

I then sealed the letter and handed it over to the Mayor of Dorchester, who was going to a parliament at Westminster to answer another of the king's interminable requests for more money for the French wars. The mayor had just received his brief from the town burgesses who had gathered in the great tap-room of the inn where I was staying. The mayor agreed to take the letter when I approached him after the meeting, and I invited him to sup with me. He was puffed out like a farm cockerel with his mission to London. He damned the wars and he damned Isabella, through whom the king could claim the throne of France and so turn Europe from the Hook of Holland to the Pyrenees into one vast battlefield.

"It's all right for the king," he confided to me, blowing a gale of ale fumes into my face, "riding out to do battle. But who profits? The seas are plagued with pirates. Markets are empty. The fields are stripped of corn and beasts, as well as the men who tend them. The roads are the prey of ex-soldiers, vagabonds, and landless peasants. The king should stay at home, keep the peace and live off his own. The French crown, Paris, even France itself, not one or all of them together are worth the misery these wars have brought."

The mayor's complaints dominated our meal, but it was a

welcome change to my own fears and worries. The next day I left him and his little town, surprised at such vehemence, but on my journey through the countryside, I saw what he meant. Fields which should have been ploughed lay brown and fallow. Meadows were devoid of livestock. Villages were full of women and old men while roving bands of outlaws terrorised the countryside. Twice I was attacked with stones and arrows and I only escaped unscathed due to being mounted.

Five days after leaving Dorchester, I reached Yeovil in Somerset, where I learnt to my delight that the sheriff was Sir Thomas Tweng, who was busy holding the shire court at Taunton Castle. You have probably never heard of Sir Thomas, Richard. He is a simple country knight but a close friend of the king and one of his confidants in the 1330 plot to overthrow Mortimer. If anyone knew anything about Guerney and Maltravers, it would be Sir Thomas. I hurried on to Taunton and arrived exhausted at The Corn Stook which lies on the outskirts of the town, virtually under the huge walls of the great castle.

The following morning I hired one of the ostlers to take a message up to the castle, begging for immediate audience with Sir Thomas on business concerning the king. The ostler returned to inform me that he had delivered my message to the captain of the morning watch, and so I sat back and waited. The day passed and evening found me still sitting near the inn fire, anxious for a summons or a reply. I had almost despaired when the door of the inn was thrown open as a huge, pot-bellied man swept in. The landlord's subservient attitude told me that this was Tweng. He ignored the bobbing servants and swung his gaze around the room and squinted at me through the poor light.

"Beche," he bellowed, "are you the damned clerk who wants to see me?"

I nodded and rose to meet him. "Sit down, man," he rumbled, as he slumped into the chair opposite me, his huge frame filling it to overflowing. He mopped a huge, bald head and inspected me intently.

"My apologies for so tardy a reply to your message," he shouted, for all to hear. "That is why I came to see you myself, only too glad to get out of that damned, stuffy castle. Well," he continued, unfastening the clasps of his cloak, "what can I do for you?"

He waved away my letters of introduction and so I told him about my investigations and my need for further information about Edward II's murderers, Guerney, Maltravers and Ockle.

"The first two were Somerset knights," I pointed out, "hence my presence in Taunton."

Tweng pursed his lips and played with the hilt of his sword.

"Maltravers and Ockle," he said, "fled to Germany and have never been traced. Guerney is dead. He died ten years ago while I was bringing him from Italy."

I almost dropped with surprise. "You mean to say," I exclaimed, "that one of the murderers was found? Did he confess? Why did the king not tell me?"

"Tush, man," Tweng replied, "there's no need to get excited. True," Tweng nodded, "Guerney was found and arrested, but he refused to confess to anything before he died. I admit his death was an embarrassment. The king was furious though he understood that I was not at fault; hence my appointment as sheriff here. It's a rewarding post, as well as a convenient listening point for any rumours about Guerney's colleague in murder, Ockle. Look!" he exclaimed, "surely the king has mentioned it to you?"

I thought hard. Had Edward deliberately kept such information from me? I was on the point of saying he had not when I remembered Edward specifically telling me at Windsor that the hunt for his father's murderers was a job for others. "Yes," I replied, "he might have mentioned something."

"Good!" Tweng exclaimed. "Then let me give you the details about Guerney." He took a deep draught from the tankard I had placed on the table before him and settled back to talk. "Thomas Guerney and William Ockle were all judged regicides and traitors at the November parliament of 1330. Yet it is essential to realize that although Maltravers is associated with Edward II's imprisonment, only Thomas Guerney and William Ockle, his valet, were specifically accused of the king's murder. Indeed, my interest was always with Guerney, not Ockle, for where the former went, the latter was bound to follow. Be that as it may, Guerney was always regarded as the principal murderer." Sir Thomas stopped to clear his throat before continuing, "In the summer of 1331, two Spanish merchants with connections at the English court recognized Guerney in Burgos and successfully petitioned King Alphonso of Spain to have him detained. They then informed our king, who began extradition proceedings, but before they were compiled, Guerney escaped. One of the king's squires, a Spaniard named Egidius, was already in Spain, trying to persuade the authorities to deliver Guerney up. When he escaped, Egidius devoted all his energies to the pursuit. He failed to capture Guerney, but he did arrest two of the king's guards at Berkeley, John Tully and Robert Linelle. These he took back to England and," Sir Thomas paused to draw diagrams in the spilt pools of wine, "they were questioned."

I gathered from his pause that the fugitives had been tortured, which is contrary to common law. I realized that this was not the time for legal niceties and pressed him to continue.

He told me that these two had been of little use, apart from further information regarding others of the king's guards, all of whom were rounded up and questioned, although little came of it.

"Then," Sir Thomas continued a little more briskly, "on 16 January, 1333, I was with the king at York, when a report was brought in from William de Cornwall, one of the royal agents in the Kingdom of the Two Sicilies. According to this, Guerney had been seen there and the king immediately commissioned me to go to Naples to apprehend him. Preparations took about ten days and, accompanied by a small retinue, I sailed from Sandwich. We had good winds and docked at Genoa on 10 February. There the cog left us for active service in the Channel, while our party hired horses and travelled south to Naples."

"We arrived about the beginning of March and, having observed the usual protocol, John de la Haye, the seneschal of the town, handed Guerney over to us. I remember being shocked by his ragged appearance but, after a shave and a new set of clothes, he didn't look too bad. I had met Guerney many times during the reign of Edward II. He was a cocky bastard then and he hadn't changed. He said he was glad to be going back to England. Glad! I reproached him as a regicide, but he merely smiled and said he had news that would set all Europe by its ears. After that, he refused to speak about Edward's death at Berkeley."

Sir Thomas turned and bellowed to the landlord to bring candles and ale. "Anyway," he continued, "we set sail from Naples in the last week of March and landed at Couloures in Aragon on the east coast of Spain. I thought it best to cross northern Spain, through the Pyrenees, and so enter the English duchy of Gascony, rather than risk a perilous sea voyage up the Bay of Biscay. So, at Couloures, I hired mules and horses and also obtained the necessary passes to cross

Aragon and Castile. Our journey was an uneventful one, until Guerney fell ill. Nothing serious at first, just gripes in the belly, but by the time we reached Bordeaux in Gascony, he was dead." Tweng then broke off his narrative and stared hard at his thick, stubby fingers.

"I know what you're thinking, Master Beche. His death does seem very convenient and so it was judged at the time. There are stories that he was killed to protect certain people in England, not just the queen mother." Sir Thomas looked at me intently. "There's no foundations for such lies. I was especially charged by the king to look after Guerney and I took along two physicians just in case he did fall ill, yet even they could do nothing to save him. The rest of the voyage was quickly over. Guerney's body was preserved in spirits and we sailed from Bordeaux to Sandwich. The king himself inspected the corpse, and having commended me for my efforts, ordered Guerney's remains to be buried in unconsecrated ground. That's it, Master Clerk. A long, fruitless search, which resulted in nothing." Sir Thomas smiled at me mirthlessly. "I'm not surprised His Grace did not inform you about such details for they are of little importance."

I was deeply disappointed by Tweng's account. Guerney was dead. Maltravers and Ockle had disappeared and if the king's agents had failed to pick up their tracks in fourteen years, then what chance had I?

Tweng, however, had not yet finished. "What do you think, Master Clerk?" he asked. "Do you think Guerney was murdered?"

I realized the poor man, for all his bombast, still had doubts himself. I asked about the retinue which he had taken on his journey.

"Twenty in all, not counting myself," he replied. "The two physicians, but they never approached him till he fell ill.

Then there were six valets who took care of our needs and twelve royal sergeants, all volunteers."

"Did any of these ever speak to the prisoner?"

"Yes," Sir Thomas replied quickly. "A big thick-set fellow, very capable with his hands. A good soldier, like any Scot. He used to have regular conversations with Guerney, but when I questioned them separately, I found they had both done service in the Scottish campaign of 1328. "Anyway," he shrugged, "the man's innocent of any guilt, as I had sent him on to Gascony the day before Guerney fell ill."

I didn't really listen to anything else Sir Thomas said. The word 'Scot' rang like a bell in my brain and I knew that whatever Tweng might suspect, Guerney had been murdered. I let Sir Thomas ramble on.

"Has the king recently ordered you to resume your efforts to capture Maltravers?" I asked.

"Yes," Sir Thomas replied, "during the last six months, the king has paid me extra sums to hire spies, but the money's wasted. I have thirty agents working in the duchies of Germany and not one has made the slightest progress."

I murmured words of consolation, promising to share any information I unearthed. For my part, it was a lie from the start. I intended to leave Sir Thomas chasing his will-o'-the-wisps in Europe, while I tracked down Michael the Scot.

Tweng, however, seemed to have little inclination to let me go.

"Look, Master Clerk," he explained, "you're in this as deep as I am and you seem just as confused. I have drawn up a file of documents on the late king's imprisonment. Perhaps you would like to inspect them. They're at the castle."

It would have been churlish to spurn such an offer and I

was greedy for any fresh information, so I offered to present myself at the castle the next morning. Sir Thomas bluffly rejected this and told me he would bring the file down personally. He then rose, nodded good-night and swept out.

The next morning I rose early, bribed the landlord for the best table near the window and obtained the loan of a portable writing tray. I had scarcely finished my preparations when Sir Thomas joined me, bearing a thick roll of vellum.

"This is everything I know about Edward II's death," he announced. "Look through it and see if any of it can be of help to you."

I insisted on buying him his breakfast, and while he ate it I unrolled the roll of vellum and began to move swiftly through the entries. Most of them were immediately recognizable as items I had already discovered, but one did catch my eye. This was the confession of Tully, one of the sentries at Berkeley Castle during Edward II's imprisonment. The man was evidently a common foot-soldier and was innocent of any involvement in the late king's death. Tully, however, had been on castle guard the night Dunheved attacked. According to Tully, he and the other soldiers were assigned only to the battlements, the inner bailey being the preserve of Ockle and Guerney. On the night of Dunheved's attack, Tully had been completely surprised as the assailants had entered the castle by a sewer which ran from the moat into the inner bailey. Consequently (and I took note of the wording), Tully only knew of the attack when he heard the sound of the uproar behind him in the inner bailey and saw Dunheved's men break and flee towards him on the man main castle wall. What was most significant was Tully's claim that Dunheved's men actually got into the castle and were escaping before being either cut down or forced to surrender. This contradicted earlier statements that Dunheved's gang were stopped at the walls. I copied Tully's confession down and returned the roll to Sir Thomas, who had been anxiously watching me.

"Is that all you need?"

"Yes," I replied, "and now, Sir Thomas, I must say goodbye."

We shook hands, promising that we would share information. I told him where he could contact me and I walked into the yard of the inn and shouted for my horse. Sir Thomas followed me into the frosty yard and watched as I mounted.

"Master Beche?" he asked. "Why do you think the king informed neither of us that the other was involved in this business?"

The same question had occurred to me and I gave him the same conclusion I had reached. The king had assigned me to write a history of his late father's reign, not the task of tracking down his father's murderers. Tweng looked about as satisfied as I felt at such an explanation, but time was pressing. We both agreed to keep our meeting together a secret. I nodded farewell and continued my departure.

My journey back was uneventful. I reached the capital this morning and I was in Bread Street when the bells of St Paul were calling for the midday Angelus. I left my horse in the hands of the ostler of The Green Man and entered its cool darkness. The place fell strangely quiet. At first, I thought it was due to my dusty appearance until Noyon, the landlord, bustled up and, avoiding my eyes, told me to sit. I gathered from his face that he brought bad news, common knowledge to all, but affecting only me.

"It's Kate, Master Beche," Noyon answered my look. "She's dead, murdered three nights ago. She was found with her throat cut, near St Martin-le-Grand."

The coldness which numbed me then still lingers on. I asked if there was a culprit, but Noyon was uncertain. He told me a huge, black-faced man with a foreign accent had been making enquiries about me the day before Kate's death. "Perhaps it was he, but the coroner was unable to question him, as he vanished as mysteriously as he had come. This," Noyon added, "was found in one of her pockets."

It was a piece of parchment with the words *"mortui mortuos saepeliant"* – "let the dead bury the dead" – and I remembered that the she-wolf had given me similar advice at Castle Rising.

I thanked Noyon and stumbled back to my lodgings, where I lay staring for hours at the parchment. I have it now, neatly folded in my wallet, and I intend to return it to the Scot. Somehow or other, he murdered Guerney; he has tried to kill me once and probably came to London to finish the job. When he found me absent, he must have decided to kill Kate and terrorize me into silence. That old bitch, Isabella, works the man like a puppet but if I cannot reach her, then I will be satisfied with the Scot. I beg you, Richard, not to write with texts to leave vengeance to the Lord. By the time this letter reaches you, such vengeance will have been carried out. God keep you. Written at Bread Street 11 April, 1346.

Letter Seven

Edmund Beche to Richard Bliton, greetings. You must not think I ended my last letter with vain, empty threats. I was distraught at Kate's death. Indeed, I still am. I did not love the girl, but I feel sorrow and guilt that such an innocent should suffer because of me. The morning after my return to London, I visited her small, forlorn grave and wept unashamedly. I ordered a stone cross to be placed there and paid a fee for masses to be said by a Chancery priest.

I also settled other affairs in London before using the king's commission to draw further monies. The Exchequer clerk told me that one day I would have to account for it all. He looked even angrier when I said that the king had received more than he could ever give me. I left my old mare at The Green Man and bought a splendid beast, more suited for a knight than a clerk at the chancery, but past experience had already shown that my life could depend on the speed of a horse. I then fastened on my sword and dagger and left the capital for Cambridge and King's Lynn.

It seemed so empty to leave without a kiss from Kate, and for the first time in my life I felt a loneliness that was more than a mere state of mind. I have no kin. My parents died working a small farm on the Pennines to send their only son to Oxford. Kate is gone and you, Richard, are locked away in your monastery. As I rode out of London, I felt that only the task I had now set myself was worth living for.

The horse I had bought proved its worth and after four days' steady riding, with only a few stops for food and rest, I arrived once again at The Sea Barque. Naturally, I was greeted with surprised joy by the fraternity which haunt that place and no small embarrassment by the landlord. He confessed that he had kept my saddle and bags but sold the sumpter-pony as he thought I had gone forever. I improved my standing by telling him to keep the price he had made as I had now found employment with a rich London merchant. I used this as my excuse for my swift departure from King's Lynn the first time and explained that I was on my master's business to Kingston-upon-Hull.

The man laughed and shook his head in disbelief at my good fortune. "Thank God, Master Beche. We thought some evil had befallen you."

"How is that?" I said, although I suspected the answer even before I'd heard the landlord's reply.

"It was Michael the Scot, the old queen's man. He came here a few days after you left and made inquiries about a clerk fitting your frame. We knew it was you, but we kept quiet, though we wondered how you had crossed swords with the lout."

I glibly explained that I had tried to seek employment with the old queen, but had been turned back by the Scot, whom I had roundly cursed. The landlord then told me to be wary and lie low. I grimly decided to follow his advice for I was determined to strike before my enemy knew I was back.

A few discreet inquiries on my part revealed that Michael the Scot had one weakness. Now and again he came alone to King's Lynn to visit a young widow called Mistress Launge, who lived alone outside the city walls. According to common report, Michael was hot for her as she was cold towards him. The ruffian's fruitless suit was common knowledge and gleefully watched by all and sundry.

I decided to call upon Mistress Launge and found her at home in her small, neat two-storeyed house which sits on the border of the royal forests which surrounded King's Lynn. At first, she was reluctant even to let me in, but when I hastily exclaimed I knew of a way to rid her of Michael the Scot, the door was flung wide open in welcome. She was a small nut-brown girl with lustrous black hair, blue eyes and regular features. She looked as soft as a young spring doe, but I discovered she hated the Scot as much as I did. Sitting in her small kitchen, warmed by a sparkling fire and lit by the rays of a watery sun, she told me about herself and the Scot. How she had been married young to an elderly mercer, a kindly man, who only survived the marriage by six months. For a while, she lived the life of a respectable widow until the Scot had seen her at last year's Michaelmas Fair. Since then, he had pursued and pestered her like some imp from hell, threatening and coaxing her to enter his bed. She had no relatives, no men folk to protect her,whilst he stood high in the old queen's favour. So far she had resisted him, but she was becoming terrified of what he might do. I commiserated with her and then, little by little, explained why I had visited her, basing my story on half-truths; how the Scot had attacked me in London, then in spite murdered my betrothed. I gently stroked her hatred for the Scot, until it overcame the terror in which she held him and so together we laid our plot.

The next day I visited the woods outside King's Lynn and, having found the site I was looking for, I returned to my chamber at the inn. I stayed there until dusk, then I dressed in my darkest clothes, blackened my hands and face, and quietly led my saddled horse out of The Sea Barque. The widow was waiting for me and nervously announced that all was ready. She had combed her hair and wore a kirtle of scarlet which emphasized her small, round breasts and narrow waist. I repeated my plan, received her assurances and then went up to her chamber, where I hid myself behind the arras which ran alongside the wall at the foot of the bed. Here I found the dagger and club I had ordered to be concealed. Satisfied that all was well, I settled down to wait. After a while, I heard knocking on the downstairs door and then the gruff voice of the Scot announcing himself. The house became silent, broken only by the sound of faint laughter and the clash of cups. Suddenly, there was a squeal and a thumping on the stairs, then the chamber door flung open and Michael the Scot walked through, carrying a struggling Mistress Launge. Without a word, he flung the woman on the great bed and began to unfasten the lacing of his breeches. Once stripped, he flung himself on to the unfortunate woman, his great hands thrusting under her petticoat while he buried his face into her long neck. I waited for a few seconds more, slipped from behind the arras and brought my club down on to the man's head with a resounding thwack. He jerked, groaned and slipped unconscious to the floor. Mistress Launge sufficiently recovered herself to help me bind and gag the unconscious man and then drag him downstairs. I went outside and brought my horse from the rear of the house, and, having assured ourselves that all was quiet, we dragged the Scot out and bound him across my saddle. I whispered my farewells to the girl and promised that she would see neither me nor the Scot again.

I then took the reins of my horse and headed for the place in the woods I had marked earlier in the day. It was about a mile from the track, a small moonlit clearing which fringed an evil-smelling marsh. I unhorsed my captive and, having spread-eagled him, lashed and pegged his hands and feet to the ground. He struggled to rise, but I kicked him between the legs and told him to keep quiet. He peered up at me. "Ah, it is the clerk," he grunted. "Come for vengeance? Where's Mistress Launge? Not here? Ah, well, there'll be another day."

"For her and for me," I replied, "there might be. You're never going back and your queen, the French bitch, will have to find herself another mongrel." In the light of the torch, I saw his fear. He struggled against the cords and gazed wildly into the surrounding darkness.

"You're not to slay me, Master Beche," he gasped. "You're a clerk, I'll be missed." My look must have only confirmed his fears and he began to shout at me in a mixture of pleas, oaths and threats which ended in a shriek as I drove my dagger into his hand.

"Did you kill the girl in London?"

"Yes."

"Why?"

"As a warning to you to leave the past alone."

"Is that why you attacked me?" I drove my dagger into his other hand.

"Yes," he shrieked.

"And what about Edward II? Did you have anything to do with his death?"

"No," Again I pressed the dagger into the fleshy part of his right hand, causing him to shriek and writhe.

"God is my witness," he shouted, "but I know nothing. I only do what the queen orders."

"Did she order Guerney's execution?" I asked.

He nodded and quickly told me that in 1333 he was acting as Isabella's spy at her son's court. When the king heard that Guerney was in Naples, Isabella had ordered him to volunteer for service in the force sent out to apprehend him. Once Guerney was captured, he was to gain his confidence

by promising Guerney the queen's support and protection
once he was back in England.

"Why?" I asked.

"To see what he knew."

"About what?"

"Her husband's death."

"Why was the queen so interested?"

"I don't know."

"Did you gain anything?"

The Scot nodded. "Only a little. Guerney said he had
news which would set all Christendom by its ears. When I
pressed him for details, he merely smiled, although on one
occasion he did say, 'Kent was right; he knew all along.'"

I made him repeat this and asked if there was anything
else.

"No," the Scot replied. "I carried out Madam's orders
and began to lace his water with a poison she had given me.
It was a rare Italian mixture, which only acted over a
number of days. It led to cramps, pains and eventually a
coma, from which the victim never awakes. I did that before
we arrived at Boulogne, but that's all I know. I swear it."
The man looked at me beseechingly, but I remembered Kate
and drove my dagger straight into his heart.

So, Richard, I have taken a life. Edmunde Beche, the
student who would vomit if he saw a dog go under a cart.
Murder? It was self-defence, justice for Kate and peace for
many others. He brought about his own death and I bear no
scruples for doing what the public hangman gets paid to do
more slowly.

But the purpose of this letter is not to moralize. Once the
body had stopped twitching, I loaded it with stones, cut the
ropes, then dragging it to the edge of the marsh, threw it in.
It sank without trace, as did the knife and cords I threw in
after. I then washed away all traces of blood in a nearby

brook, mounted my horse and rode out of the wood. I skirted King's Lynn and struck south for Cambridge. By the time I reached the small village of Burwell, I felt so tired that I hobbled my horse and fell asleep on a bed of bracken.

I woke about midday the next morning and pressed on for Cambridge, which I reached the same evening. The halls and colleges were all closed, so I lodged in a traveller's rest just inside the city walls. There I tried to make sense out of Guerney's reference to Kent. I decided it must be an allusion to Edmund, Earl of Kent, half-brother to Edward II and uncle to the present king. He had joined Isabella and Mortimer against Edward II but then fell from favour and was executed in 1329. I had made a rough copy of the chronicle of St Paul's description of the four-year reign of Mortimer and Isabella, and recollection of the bizarre details surrounding Kent's death sent me feverishly rummaging in my saddle-bag. I unrolled the greasy parchment and found a story which corroborated my suspicions about Edward II's imprisonment and death at Berkeley.

According to the chronicler of St Paul's (who based himself on official records), in 1329 certain men came and told Edmund of Kent that Edward his brother was not dead but still alive in the Castle of Corfe. Edmund travelled as fast as he could to that castle and had a long conversation with John Deveril, the constable there. Kent begged the constable to tell him whether Edward II was imprisoned there and, if he was, he begged to see him. Deveril replied that Edward was alive, but he dare not show him to anyone without the express command of Queen Isabella and Sir Roger Mortimer. Whereupon the Earl of Kent gave Deveril a letter for his brother, but the constable immediately went to London and delivered it to Mortimer and Isabella. They then used the letter against Kent, claiming that he was stirring up sedition in the country with lies that his brother was still alive. They had him arrested, tried and judged as a traitor at a parliament swiftly assembled at Winchester. Once sentence was passed, Kent was immediately taken out and executed by the common hangman of the city.

After I had finished reading, I kept thinking about Guerney's words, "Kent was right, he knew all along." I immediately realized what he meant. The chronicler had maintained that the story about Edward II being at Corfe Castle was a deliberate lie, concocted by Mortimer to trap Kent. But why? The earl would never have accepted such a story, unless he had good reason to believe his half-brother was still alive somewhere. On the other hand, Mortimer would never have gone to such lengths to trap Kent, a nonentity, unless he knew that the earl had seen through one of the greatest deceptions ever practised in this realm. The body buried at Gloucester in October 1327 was not Edward II. I believe that Edward II escaped from Berkeley during Dunheved's attack and a corpse was substituted for the royal burial.

The Dunheved gang, it must be remembered, were only detected after they left the inner bailey where Edward II had been kept. They probably intended to use the secret exit from the castle but, once they were discovered, Dunheved must have urged the now free Edward to flee while he covered his escape. Dunheved's men were either wiped out there and then, or rounded up very soon afterwards and quietly murdered in prison. Isabella and Mortimer must have frantically searched for the deposed king but, when this proved fruitless, decided to cover up the escape with a mock burial. This was the only way to discredit Edward, if and when, he re-emerged on to the political scene. The cover-up was easy. Remember, Richard, my conversation with Novile, the loquacious steward at Berkeley? He pointed out that the body of Pellet, the guard killed during the Dunheved attack, was preserved in spirits for conveyance to Bordeaux. I believe that this corpse was never sent, but lies buried in the royal tomb at Gloucester Cathedral.

Why was the deception so successful? Well, Novile described how the corpse was laid out. Only the face was exposed and it is quite simple to see how people believed it was the face of a dead king. First, the corpse was kept at Gloucester, away from the prying eyes of the court physician, and attended to by an old hag. Secondly, if anyone did notice anything strange, suspicion could easily be allayed. Edward II (as the effigy at Gloucester illustrates) usually wore a long, curly beard but, according to Novile, the hair was covered by the cowl of the shroud, whilst the face had been shaved for burial. Moreover, those who saw the corpse would accept the radical changes usually imposed by death: the pallor of the skin, the bloodless lips, the sharpness of the features and the sunken cheeks. These would be even more readily accepted for the corpse had been embalmed and above ground for two months before burial. In a word, people believed what they came to see, a dead king laid out for burial. How the Earl of Kent saw through the deception is unknown; the chronicle of St Paul's says that certain men "informed" him, but his doubts may well have begun when he paid his last respects to "Edward's" corpse at Gloucester.

Isabella must have found out about these doubts and enticed Kent into treason and summary execution by feeding him false information about Edward II's whereabouts. I believe she would have eventually got rid of Guerney, Maltravers and Ockle. I know she tried to kill me, and will probably try again. She realizes that I saw through her tissue of lies. I do not even believe her story about the embalmed heart. I suspect it belonged to Mortimer, not Edward II.

Of, course, Edward may have been recaptured and secretly

killed, but I think not. First, Mortimer confessed to Orleton that he had not murdered Edward II. Secondly, Isabella's conduct proves that her husband not only escaped but may still be alive and well. She hides in a secluded fortress and hires a private army to protect her from a vengeful husband. Every day must be a nightmare, wondering what horror stalks the wet dark woods of Norfolk.

A few things still puzzle me. Does our present king know about this? I think he suspects but how did he find out? And why is the matter now so urgent and secretive? After all, the world believe that Edward II was killed over fifteen years ago and now lies rotting under his marble tomb at Gloucester. All I do know is that the great ones of this world do not like their secrets revealed. To be frank, I fear for my own safety, and I am only going to reveal all I know when the circumstances favour it.

A bizarre story, dear Richard, but I do believe that Edward II escaped from Berkeley and I intend to find out why and what happened to him. I have other tasks to accomplish. I cannot tell you what they are, for as a churchman you would surely object. I beseech you to keep this quiet, even from your confessor. I intend to send this and future letters concealed in personal gifts for you. My messengers are always trustworthy men, well paid for their services. I hope you do not object. Your knowing about what I do is a guarantee for my own safety. God keep you, Richard, and pray for me, for I feel as if I sorely need it. Written at Cambridge, 29 May, 1346.

Letter Eight

Edmund Beche to Richard Bliton, Prior of Croyland Abbey, greetings. I reached Gloucester a week after leaving Cambridge and, apart from dropping off my horse through sheer fatigue, losing my way and, on one occasion, riding for my life from a group of outlaws, my journey was fairly uneventful. As the poet sang, "Sumer is i-cumen," the countryside lay like the garden of Eden and I momentarily forgot Kate's death, Michael the Scot and even the grim task which lay before me.

When I reached Gloucester, I lodged at the Cross Keys, a small tavern in one of the many back streets near the city's west gate. I paid for a month's board, arranged for the stabling of my horse and then once more visited the cathedral. I devoted particular attention to the position of Edward II's tomb which lies on the left side of the high altar, about four roods in distance from the great north wall. I went outside and was relieved to find that the exterior of the north wall facing the tomb was not only free of other buildings, but fringed by an overgrown cemetery strewn with clipped stone crosses and choked with weeds and briar bushes. Using the last window of the north wall as a bearing, I measured out ten paces to a particularly dense clump of gorse and judged that I was standing directly opposite the tomb. I repeated the whole performance a number of times till I was certain and then returned to the Cross Keys to saddle my horse.

I rode out of the city's west gate and took the road leading to Monmouth until I came to the bridge which spanned the meeting of the Wye and Severn Rivers. Across this lies the cool, green darkness of the Forest of Dean, and I had only penetrated half a mile into it when a party of royal verderers appeared. They asked my business and I flourished the now yellowing royal warrant. They carefully inspected the royal seal and became only too anxious to answer my queries about the whereabouts of the nearest mine-works.

Ever since the time of the Romans, the Forest of Dean has been quarried for its iron, tin and coal, and there are still workings throughout the area. Following the directions of the verderers, I came across the nearest in a huge clearing, dotted with wooden huts and littered with heaps of rubble, disused plankings and round iron pitchers. Over all hung a thick, heavy smoke which weaved across the clearing and into the trees beyond, fouling the air with the stench of burning pitch. I was approached by a small, wiry man, dressed in boots, moleskin breeches and leather jerkin, all of which were covered in dirt and dried crusts of tar. He introduced himself as the mine's overseer. I showed him the king's commission but placated his evident concern by pointing out that I was not there to snoop, but merely to satisfy my curiosity. I explained that I was a keen student of engineering, being attached to the office of the king's Surveyor of Royal Works.

The man seemed satisfied and took me on a tour of his domain, just as Virgil led Dante through the nethermost parts of hell. He answered my questions about vents, shafts, tunnels, stays and the use of guide ropes. My brain became bemused by all the dangerous intricacies of mining. Eventually, the tour was finished. I thanked the man and gave him a mark for his service which left him speechless with gratitude. I mounted and rode to the nearest pool to drink and bathe the dust from my face.

The city gates were closed when I reached Gloucester just after dusk, and only a great deal of argument and a small amount of silver persuaded the watch to open the postern gate and let me through. That night I slept so soundly that it was midday before I left the Cross Keys. I walked up the dirty cobbled street to the City Cross and the multi-coloured striped awnings of the market stalls which surround it. I wandered across the great square, my hand on my purse and my eyes wary of the cut-purses and thieves who flocked to such places like all the plagues of Egypt.

The warm spring weather had brought the crowds swarming in to buy gewgaws, food, clothes, or even potions from the quacks who wandered the countryside selling their elixirs. There was a mangy bear being taunted by even mangier dogs, while all around the pit, jugglers and tumblers entertained the crowd. I had become so immersed in the king's private affair that I realized how little time I had taken to relax and enjoy myself in that most enjoyable of occupations – sitting in the sun and watching the world go by. I then thought of my walks with Kate through the markets of London, and this brought me back to grim reality.

I quickly went around the necessary stalls; from one I bought a number of large, thick, hempen sacks, from another, two small pickaxes and shovels, three hundred yards of thick cord, and a stack of short wooden planks. I bundled all my purchases into one of the sacks and then returned to the cathedral churchyard, where I buried them beneath the rubble of a collapsed tomb. The rest of the day I spent at the inn, eating, dozing and waiting for nightfall. When the cries of the watch announced that the city was asleep, I quickly snatched some old clothes and returned to the graveyard. Apart from the screech of a hunting owl, all was quiet. I quickly changed my clothes, dragged out a pick and shovel and began to dig on the spot I had marked the day before. The earth was soft and loose and soon I was using the planks to create a primitive shaft, like the ones I had seen in the mines of the Forest of Dean. Once I had judged this to be deep enough, I began to carve out a tunnel, gathering the rubble into the sacks. Once a sack was full, I strengthened the tunnel with more wood and clambered out to empty it into a ditch which ran along the far end of the cemetery. I began the task with vigour but, by dawn, I had only emptied three sacks from the tunnel and I was aching in every part of my body. My hair was full of dirt and my hands, so used to the tender work of the Chancery, were sore and chapped. When the stars began to disappear, I judged it was time to leave. I covered my tunnel with planks and then replaced the surface sods I had so carefully removed. After that, I stripped, wiped my body with some wet rags and, dressed in my usual robes with a hood covering my head, I walked back to the inn for food and sleep.

By now, Richard, you must have realized that I intend to break into Edward II's tomb. I do not believe it is sacrilege; the real desecration took place seventeen years ago when Isabella and her paramour duped Lords, Church and Commons by staging a mockery of a royal funeral. I needed to open the tomb, not only to expose their sacrilege, but to silence a nagging doubt behind the king's motives in ordering this inquiry.

The tunnelling took two exhausting weeks and suffered many setbacks. Sometimes the tunnel collapsed and, on one occasion, I was suddenly overwhelmed by a fear that the earth would close in on me and stop my breath. Time and

time again the dead met me, the eyeless skulls and the empty
skeletons of the countless bodies buried in the soil through
which I ploughed. I prayed that Christ would understand
my desecration, but the empty eye-sockets, glaring at me in
the light of my small flint light, made me dread the work I
had begun. Sometimes, as I returned to the inn, I felt as if
these disturbed dead pattered beside me to fill my dreams
with haunting nightmares.

My growing paleness, coupled with the strange hours I
kept, eventually aroused the suspicions of the landlord. I
only silenced him with the king's warrant and a handful of
silver. Nevertheless, I wished my business was over. So far,
my labours have gone undisturbed, as graveyards are left
well alone, even in daylight. Yet I was weary and tired and
becoming anxious at my growing mounds of rubble. I was
also afraid that my frequent purchases of planks and sacking
might arouse curiosity. If I was caught, I could expect little
mercy. Grave-robber or witch, whatever the verdict, I would
surely hang and the king, who knew nothing of what I was
doing, could never save me. Twelve days after beginning my
work, I was beneath the cathedral wall. The tunnel I had
dug was now about the height and width of one prostrate
man. I had used a guide rope to ensure it ran straight, but I
had met so many obstacles and the light was so poor that I
strongly suspected that I had gone off course. Nevertheless,
I was pleased with my work which I had planned on what I
had learned in the Forest of Dean, as well as my meagre
military knowledge about the mining of castle walls. After
another week's work, I managed to wriggle under the
curtain wall and began to hack at the sandy soil beneath the
cathedral flag-stones. The morning I thought I should have
reached the tomb still found me digging, and so I decided to
tunnel to my left. Another night passed and, at last, I found
what I was looking for – a tunnel similar to the one I had

dug. I managed to clear the loose rubble away until I reached solid rock. I pushed my torch towards this, almost singeing my face, to find a man-made wall of dullish red brick. I probed the section directly facing me and loosened enough bricks to clear a small passage. Once through, I emptied my pouch into my lap, found a flint and lit the two rush-lights I had brought. I knew I was in some form of cavern for, despite the heavy mustiness which cloyed my throat, I could feel space on every side of me. The rush-lights flared to reveal a small chamber, a complete square with walls of brick about two yards high. Above this lay the flagstones of the cathedral and the gorgeous memorial to King Edward II, and, on the floor, directly in the centre of the chamber I had entered lay a long oaken chest. It was about four feet high and about the same across. I fixed the rush-lights in two of the sockets on either side of it and I was not surprised to find the lid easy to move, though it creaked as I pushed it aside.

A sharp acrid smell forced me to cough and it was some time before I lifted one of the rush-lights. It showed a crumbling, wooden, lidless coffin, lined with the remnants of fur and samite and covered with the shards of a white, gauze-like material. Beneath this lay a skeleton, the body perfectly straight, though the skull was askew like the head of a hanged man. Praying softly, I removed the gauze to examine further. Precious rings, which had once probably adorned the fingers, winked in the light and, at the bottom of the coffin, I found the gold pieces which must have been pressed into the eye-sockets. I then examined the skull and found a deep fracture which seemed to be the work of man, rather than the slow rot of the grave. Was this the guard Pellet's fatal wound? I leaned forward into the musty coffin to replace the skull and yelled with horror when the soggy wood at the bottom of the coffin split to reveal another, smaller, hollow-eyed skull. I crouched in terror, breathing deeply to compose myself. When I was calm again, I stood and began to clear the coffin of the skeleton and its remains. I then raised the dark, wet wood at the bottom to reveal the second skeleton. It was smaller and more decomposed than the first. The back of the skull was smashed in, the jawbone hung loose, and I immediately noticed that it was bereft of all teeth except a few yellow stumps. Who could it be? I reconstructed the list of all those who had definitely been present at the preparation of "Edward II's" body. There was one person unaccounted for. The old crone who had dressed the corpse. The skeleton would fit her frame and general description. Her death and secret burial was an ingenious way of keeping a secret. I breathed a "Miserere," replaced all as I had found it, and then made my way slowly back to the surface.

After a few days' rest, I left for London, having made sure that the shaft and tunnel under the cathedral wall were covered and sealed and all traces of my work hidden from any prying eyes. I should have felt some relief, but instead there was only growing anger. I had braved the perils of sea and land on the king's behalf, killed for him, lost my Kate because of him, and yet, the task he had assigned me was based on a tissue of lies.

You see, Richard, I broke into the tomb at Gloucester, not to examine the coffin, but to find out if someone had been there before me. They evidently had. This explains the disused tunnel, the opening into the tomb, and the unsealed coffin lid. No grave robber would have been so careful or ignored the precious stones I saw there. This could only mean it was someone with specific interest in the tomb. I believe this to be the king himself. Two factors force me to this conclusion. First, I have always wondered why the king ordered me to investigate the circumstances surrounding his father's death, some eighteen years after the event took place. Secondly, the king was at Gloucester just two weeks before he ordered me to begin my investigation. Sir Maurice Berkeley remarked on the king's interest in his father's tomb when he visited Gloucester and he, or more likely Chandos, who accompanied him, dug that small tunnel in order to inspect the corpse. The king knew that an imposter was buried at Gloucester and simply wished to verify the fact, or even check that a corpse was really buried there. Only pure chance had prevented him finding the second corpse. However, what is more important is that I reached my conclusions through hard research and the assassination of Michael the Scot. But how did the king come to know? And why had he not informed me? As I rode back to London, I decided that some other source existed which the king did not wish me to see. My investigation had never been intended to reach any conclusion, but merely to throw up some information to corroborate this source. The king has simply used me, like some pawn in a game of chess, and I wondered again about my usefulness once this game is over. What happens to royal clerks who know too much about the great ones they serve? A diplomatic mission to some far-away place? Or an unfortunate accident in a grimy, crowded London street? Not for me, Richard. I shall return to London and pursue this task until the end. I will find out what did happen to Edward II at Berkeley Castle and why it has become so important to our king. Then I shall settle undisturbed far beyond the reach of our devious monarch. But first, I had to discover the king's source of information. Hence, my journey back to the capital in the vain hope that I might discover something fresh amongst the records.

I arrived back in Bread Street to find a royal writ awaiting me, which demanded further reports on my investigation. It had been issued directly by the king and sent under the secret seal. It was dated at Bouvins in Normandy only a few days before and so I decided to ignore it for the moment. Instead I concentrated on where I could begin my search. As I sat staring at the writ I had just received, I suddenly knew where the information must lie – in the office of the secret seal, the one place expressly forbidden me by the king.

You probably know, Richard, there is the great seal in the custody of the Chancellor, and the privy seal, carried by another royal official. Both these seals are used to issue charters, letters and licences, but the secret seal is used exclusively by the king and covers any delicate or serious matter concerning himself or the kingdom. From my days in the Chancery, I knew that the office of the secret seal had a record depository behind locked doors in the Tower Muniment Room. Documents stored there are usually handed over in sealed caskets by the Chancellor, or even the king himself. No other person is allowed access to them without their express permission. I determined to break into the record room but I knew that I could not use the king's commission, as it was now considerably dated and not specific enough to fool a Chancery official.

I decided to resume my search at the Muniment Room and cultivate the venerable clerk in charge of the secret seal records – John Luttreshall. The latter is a high-ranking official, a man grown old in the service of the royal administration. He knew me by sight and, with a little flattery on my part, I soon turned his acquaintance into a friendship. We established a custom of sharing a wine-skin after the day's work when the other clerks were gone. John would grow expansive and gabble like a chicken about what he had done, whilst I sat open-mouthed in pretended astonishment at his petty achievements.

Yesterday evening I laced John's wine with poppy-juice that I had bought from an apothecary. The old man quickly slumped, head on hands, into a deep sleep and I immediately went to work. I removed the chain of keys from his belt and opened the locks on the door to the secret seal records. Once through, I lit some tapers which revealed a long, low-vaulted chamber with white walls reaching up to a black-raftered ceiling. I realized that the depository was modelled on the same system as the rest of the Muniment Room with the documents sealed in small hide-skinned trunks according to the king's regnal year. Edward III had been crowned in January 1327, and I had received my commission in his eighteenth, 1345. I found the casket for that year on a shelf near the door and, having broken the king's seal, began to work my way through its contents. There were a whole series of documents. Reports from spies and traitors at the French court, letters from the king to private individuals, and a collection of memoranda from the royal council. At last, I unrolled a small scroll bearing a broken seal I did not recognise. It was a letter from Manuel Fieschi, a clerk of the Papal Court in Avignon, and as I slowly deciphered the Norman French, my heart began to pound with excitement.

I hurried out of the chamber. John was still snoring softly, so I swiftly made a rough copy of the letter and returned it. Despite my excitement, I realized that someone would discover that the casket had been tampered with. I softened the wax of the broken seal, closed the casket lid and, pressing the seal together again, hoped that it would escape attention, at least for a while. I then relocked the chamber door, returned the keys to the still sleeping John and quickly strolled back to my house in Bread Street.

I cannot give you Fieschi's letter in full, Richard, but its contents, to use Guerney's expression, would certainly "set all Europe by its ears." Fieschi claims that Edward II had not died at Berkeley, but had escaped during the Dunheved

attack and managed to reach Ireland. From there, he had
sailed to France where he had met Fieschi at the Papal
Court. The deposed king, so Fieschi maintained, was
travelling in disguise and only revealed his identity after
being given absolution in confession, and then left the Papal
Court with the firm intention of travelling to Italy. The letter
gave no indication of his whereabouts in Italy, but
concluded with the firm hope that our present king would
determine the truth of the matter. Even more incredible is
that the letter is dated June 1345, only three months,
Richard, before the king assigned me to this inquiry.

The contents of Fieschi's letter may seem incredible, but
for me, they simply prove that Edward II was not buried at
Gloucester and our king knew this from the start. I have
spent the entire night wondering what to do next – and I
have reached several conclusions.

Item – there is no trace of our present king's instigating
any search for his father. This is understandable. Fieschi's
letter would need further substantiation before the king
began a venture which would surprise Europe. However
close he tries to keep the secret, truth will out, and rumour
spreads like the plague. I am sure that Fieschi has already
received a swift rebuttal of his report, or a substantial bribe
to keep him quiet.

Item – the letter speaks of Edward II going south to Italy.
So where would an English fugitive go in Italy? To the
north, riven by war, as well as the market for many English
merchants? Or the south, where any Englishman, as Sir
Thomas Guerney proved, soon comes to the attention of the
authorities? No, Richard, all roads lead to Rome, an ideal
place to hide. It is an independent state, filled with many
nationalities, as well as a refuge for exiles from all over
Europe.

Item – Edward II has been gone for eighteen years, yet

has never made any attempt to publicize his existence. This can only mean he wants to lead a sheltered life and the safest place for this is some monastery or friary.

Consequently, Richard, I intend to go to Rome and look for our unburied king, whatever the risks involved. I did think of visiting Fieschi, but I am sure he cannot tell me more than his letter already has, and such a move would certainly attract the attention of the king. I have drawn up a fictitious report for my royal master, a lie to fight a lie. In this cold London dawn the thought comforts me. I shall write again, written 19 July, 1346 at Bread Street.

Letter Nine

Edmund Beche to Richard Bliton, greetings. I intended to despatch this letter from Italy but circumstances, as you will see, have forced me to write again.

I enclose a letter from Sir Thomas Tweng. Please read it as it makes a most interesting revelation.

Sir Thomas Tweng to Edmund Beche, Clerk of the Chancery, greetings. I write in confidence to one who is also in pursuit of the truth, whatever that may be. Shortly after you left Taunton, one of my agents in the Low Countries, Peter Teloy, sent me an astonishing report. He had managed to track down John Maltravers, living under an assumed name near Ypres in Flanders. Teloy decided not to approach him but keep him under surveillance for a few weeks. He eventually reported that Maltravers (or "Groot" as he now called himself) was rich and entertained many of the wealthy burgesses, supporters of our king in his war against the French. Teloy could not understand this and so he started to make his own enquiries amongst the burgesses of Ypres. It finally emerged that Maltravers passed himself off as an Anglo-Flemish knight and Edward of England's special agent in Flanders! Such a position is not wholly remarkable. Maltravers was never specifically accused of the murder of Edward II. He may well have received a secret pardon in return for perpetual but comfortable exile as the king's spy in the Low Countries. However, more was to come. Teloy became friendly with the wife of one of the most important burgesses who visited Maltravers. From her Teloy learnt that "Groot" was making discreet inquiries on the whereabouts of a certain Englishman, a hunchback called William Ockle.

Maltravers (or "Groot") had narrowed his investigation down to the groups of mercenaries who were drifting south to offer their services to the highest bidder. Teloy decided to mix with these landless men, who told him a camp-fire story about an English sergeant-at-arms, one of Edward III's recruiters, being teased by a band of Flemish mercenaries. Evidently, the latter had mocked our king for hiring Germans to do his killing, while the city of Metz hired a hunchbacked Englishman to do theirs as the public hangman.

Teloy realized that their description of the hunchback fitted Ockle and so he immediately travelled to Metz, but he was too late. The hunchbacked Englishman had been mysteriously knifed to death two weeks before his arrival. Teloy then returned to Flanders and wrote to me reporting all he had discovered. I was angry that the king had not informed me about Maltravers. I reproached him, (as an old-time friend and colleague in the conspiracy to destroy Mortimer), for not taking me into his confidence.

The answer I received was stark and brutal. His Grace informed me that Teloy was mistaken on all points. Moreover, he was a disreputable agent, for the king had learnt that he had recently been killed in a drunken tavern brawl with some Hainaulters. I was then ordered to relinquish my task, resign my office of sheriff and assume the custody of Norham Castle. Norham! A bleak, God-forsaken spot on the Scottish March! A prince's reward for a faithful, dutiful servant. He is a worse despot than his father ever was and cunning with it. Ever since Guerney's death, I have suspected that there is something mysterious and terrible about the death of the old king at Berkeley. Teloy's report and subsequent murder – for murder it undoubtedly was – proves that.

I write to you as a bewildered old man, Master Beche. Be very wary in the task the king has assigned you. May God reward you better than he has done me. Written in haste at Taunton, 29 July, 1346.

Poor Sir Thomas. I have a strange feeling that if he ever reaches Norham alive, he will never live the year out. His letter was valuable. It underlines the seriousness of my own position. My burglary of the Secret Seal room would soon be discovered and the king may even know that Tweng had written to me. I began to make immediate preparations for my departure, selling all my moveables and trying to secure passage on a ship bound for an Italian port.

One evening after a last visit to Kate's grave, I arrived back at my lodgings to find a filthy urchin crouching outside on the cobbles. He babbled incoherently at me, thrust a grubby piece of parchment into my hand and slipped quietly away. I unrolled the scrap and read in a scrawled hand, "Edward II. In the Kirtle at Southwark. Immediately." I quickly gathered a sword, dagger and cloak from my lodgings and headed for the river bank.

While a powerful wherryman raced his little craft across the choppy Thames, I clutched my sword and wondered who had really sent the message. Southwark at night is London's answer to hell and the Kirtle Tavern has a worse reputation than the Devil himself. The wherryman must have thought I was going to visit one of the notorious brothels there. He refused to let me land until he had regaled me with advice, telling me I would get my money's worth at the Mitre, where the bawds rutted like stoats for a penny and would do anything for two. I smiled bleakly, thanked him and headed into the warren of alley-ways which ran down to the riverside. It was dark and if the rest of the city is thronged and busy during the day, then Southwark comes alive at night. Cut-throats, pick-pockets, pimps, vagabonds and outlaws roam the alleys like wolves looking for prey amongst the weak and unarmed. The streets, cluttered with filth of every kind, reek with the rot and decay of an uncleared battlefield. As I moved deeper into the darkness, the shadows which emerged from doorways slunk back as they saw the naked sword I carried. I moved forward briskly but carefully, quite aware that one stumble would bring the shadows back again. I left the riverside and the darkness became broken with the lights and noise of ale-houses and brothels. At last, I found the Kirtle, a small dingy tavern with narrow slit windows out of which poured the sound of violent roistering.

I paused, wondering whether to go in, when a hand on my elbow made me turn. She was old and bent. "A penny, sir," she hissed. "A penny and I'll tell your fortune." She pushed her face closer and I pitied the criss-cross lines on her face. Revolted by the smell from her blackened teeth. I dug into my purse and passed her a coin. She took it, her narrow eyes glittering with pleasure. As I turned back to the tavern door, she whispered, "Your future's behind you, Master."

I turned while she scurried back into the darkness. Two muffled figures, cloaked and armed with sword and dagger, stepped from the shadows. They approached slowly at a half-crouch, separating as they drew nearer.

"What do you want?" I called, biding for time.

The figures shuffled. "Hand over your sword," one of them rasped. "Our mistress would like to see you again, Master Clerk."

I realized that he meant Isabella and I knew these were her messengers and my executioners. I let my arms drop to my side. Both drew closer. When they were within striking distance, I suddenly brought up my dagger and sent it hurtling into the chest of one, while I backed and parried a blow from the other. The stricken man knelt gurgling as if he was making some obscene prayer and then fell flat on his face. His companion and I circled, looking for an opening. I am an indifferent swordsman but, *Deo gratias,* so was he, although he still had a dagger which gave him the advantage. We met, clashed, fended and parried until the sweat poured down my body. Then it was over, like many such sword fights, not with a classic stroke, but a silly mistake. My opponent slipped on some dirt, scrabbled to maintain his balance and rolled clean on to his own dagger. He died as quickly as his companion while I leaned against a door to steady myself. I realized that the message had been a trick and cursed Isabella with every filthy epithet I could think of before turning back towards the river.

The church bells told me it was past compline as I made my way from the dark wharf to my lodgings. I got no further than half-way down Bread Street before I was surrounded by mailed men-at-arms. Some carried flickering torches but their faces were hid behind coifs and basinets. They detached themselves from dark narrow alleys and doorways and stood round me, as I tried to control my fears and adopt some pathetic defensive posture. Then one of them moved out of the shadows. I noticed that he wore the royal arms of England across his tabard and, as he moved into the pool of torchlight, he removed his helmet. I was expecting

Sir John Chandos but this individual was a round-faced lad
with the bland looks of an intelligent plough-boy. He spoke
with a thick Yorkshire burr, introducing himself as Sir
Edmund Ward. He showed me a royal writ ordering him to
take me (by force if necessary) to join the king in France.
Too surprised to argue, I asked if I could gather certain
belongings from my lodgings but he merely smiled and
shook his head. He snapped his fingers, as a signal to the
escort to follow, and led me through an alleyway into the
next street where two more men-at-arms stood guarding a
line of horses.The clatter and the din of the escort woke up
the whole street. Windows were flung open and the citizens
thoroughly enjoyed themselves, shouting abuse at the
oblivious soldiery. I was unceremoniously pushed on to one
of the horses, the guard then mounted and galloped
furiously along the narrow cobbled streets, not easing their
pace till we were through the city gates. Once we were in the
country, on the road south (I guessed) to one of the Cinque
Ports, we left the beaten track to camp in a freshly harvested
field. No fire was lit, the soldiers drank from waterskins and
ate strips of dry cooked meat. They then muffled themselves
in their great cloaks and lay down to sleep. Sir Edmund
offered me food. I curtly refused though I did drink a
pannikin of water and took a thick serge cloak to keep me
warm while I slept.

   The sharp stubble and my own anxiety ensured a sleepless
night. I lay looking up at the sky, listening to the guards
patrolling the horse-lines or the small shrill cries of the
night creatures. I realized that my escort were not city
bully-boys but professional soldiers, hardened campaigners
who offered little hope of escape. I knew we were for France,
probably Normandy, where the king was said to be
launching a major offensive against the French. But why was
I going? To be questioned or to be killed? The possibility

that it could be both gave me little comfort. I wondered why the king wanted me so badly. My burglary of the secret seal records could not have been discovered so soon. But Edward, like his "dear mother" might have learnt from some source or other that my search was now pursuing a totally unexpected and very dangerous course. What or who this source was did not concern me; I spent my energies on concentrating on how to avoid the dire consequences of my coming meeting with the king. I did not intend to reveal that you, dear Richard, knew all but I hoped that if I died or disappeared, you would do something to vindicate my name.

Of course, I failed to reach a conclusion either that night or the following two days as we continued our rapid progress to the coast. I also realized that my professional escort made escape impossible. We travelled by day and camped in the open at night. Sir Edmund always ensured that I was well guarded. We rode clear of villages and inns, only stopping to buy provisions, fill the waterskins or forage for provender for the horses. Neither Sir Edmund nor his retinue spoke to me except on the second day after we left London. He curtly announced that we were going to Dover. The same evening we arrived outside that bustling port and encamped in the castle yard while Sir Edmund went into town to secure passage to France. Within hours he was back and announced that a cog, bound for Harfleur with provisions, could take us. Cursing and muttering, the escort remounted and we made our way down, along dark cobbled streets to the smelly quayside. Sir Edmund decided to return the horses to the castle, but we were ordered to take all our equipment and saddles which were heaped along with us into waiting boats and precariously rowed out to a fat squat cog, *The Saint Mary*. It was an evil-smelling barque already lying dangerously low in the water, and I prayed for a safe passage as I huddled in its fetid little hold. For once, my prayers were answered. The cog sailed on the next morning tide and the next day, late in the afternoon, we reached Harfleur. The port was now a vast munitions camp, filled with fat-bellied merchantmen from London to the Hanseatic ports on the Baltic. Sir Edmund arranged our landing and used a royal warrant to secure remounts, provisions and some vinegar-tasting wine from one of the royal purveyors stationed in the town. The place seethed like a dung-heap in summer. Troops struggled to find commanders and billets, carts jammed the narrow streets and horsemen slashed at each other as they fought to get by. Sir Edmund kept us all together and used his warrant like a wand to get through the melee. Once through the town, we entered the countryside heading south-west, so I was informed, to Valonges and Cotentin. Sir Edmund now became more relaxed and informed me that we were following the king's route across Normandy as he marched north to link up with a Flemish army against Philip VI of France.

The weather was warm. The sun was usually hidden by a haze but we felt its heat and made constant stops for water. At first, the flat dreary countryside showed little effect of Edward's march but, as we crossed the River Vire at St Lo, the war began to show itself. Burnt fields surrounded scorched deserted hamlets, farmsteads, and manor houses. Cattle and other livestock lay butchered in streams and ditches. Their black swelling bodies feeding large fat buzzing flies or, having burst, fouled the water and filled the air with such a stench that we held cloths soaked in wine across our mouths and nostrils. The horses became nervous when we caught glimpses of large bands of roving peasants who would scatter at our approach, but then dog our heels in the hope of rich pickings or bloody revenge.

At Fontenay, Sir Edmund decided on a show of force. Two men-at-arms were left to guard me while the rest swung around and began to advance at a slow trot in a wide arc across the fields we had just passed. It was just like flushing conies from the hay. Ragged peasants jumped out of ditches or from behind hedges and made pathetic attempts to escape, only to be ruthlessly cut down by the mounted men. However, Sir Edmund refused to let the escort proceed too far and when they reached the summit of a slight ridge, I saw him turn his horse and lead the troop back on to the track where he had left us. Sir Edmund announced that they had killed a good baker's dozen. The soldiers were more at ease and began to chatter and talk amongst themselves. As we approached Caen, the chatter died as we saw long columns of black smoke rising from behind the ruined town walls. We passed through where the town gates once stood only to see row upon row of charred houses, their timbers still red-hot with burning ash. We proceeded cautiously up the main street. Our horses picked their way delicately and snorted angrily at the fiery sparks blown into the air by a light evening breeze. The town square presented even worse horrors. The stone church had been badly mauled and looted but the cobbled fair-ground was strewn with dead of every age and sex. A baby lay against a horse-trough, its little skull smashed to pulp, whilst nearby its mother lay open-eyed with thick red gashes across both neck and stomach. Tradesmen lay sprawled in grotesque poses, clubs and staves still clenched in their dead hands. Those who had been stupid enough to surrender swung from improvised scaffolds, their heads twisted and lolling to one side.

I had seen enough. I leaned over my horse's neck and vomited like a drunk, then I closed my eyes until the troops were across the square and back into the winding streets. The troops, mainly hardened professionals from the northern march, remained impassive but Sir Edmund, white-faced and tight-lipped, ordered us not to stop for anything till we had left the town and re-entered the countryside. Here we began to meet roughly built hospitals for the English wounded. The latter informed us that the king was marching for the river Somme with the English fleet sailing along the Normandy coast. The English were sacking every port and hamlet on their route. The wounded also informed us that Caen had been sacked because it had refused to surrender. Sir Edmund nodded wisely, but I wondered if the little baby beside the horse-trough had understood the rules and uses of war. I said as much to Sir Edmund but all I received were dark looks and an order to dismount and help with making camp.

A week after we had landed at Harfleur we reached Poissy and turned due north, still following Edward's march to the Somme. Although I had served in a few minor campaigns a decade earlier, the carnage I witnessed on our ride through Normandy sickened me, men, women and children swinging from trees, grim monuments to Edward III's claim to the throne of France. After a while I stopped looking and hung on grimly to my tired hack. My arse and thighs ached with saddle-sores, while my tired brain seemed capable of nothing more than concentrating on the road in front of me, too tired to think of the impending interview with the King. On 20 August we reached Oisement and the rearguard of Edward's army, long dusty columns of pikemen and archers with mounted men-at-arms guarding the flanks. One of these informed our group that Philip VI with a massive French army was preparing to block the English march north. At first, Philip had tried to stop Edward from crossing the Somme but Edward had seized and held the ford at Blanchetaque and was deploying his troops on a hill outside the village of Crécy. We pressed on and, as we approached Blanchetaque, we realized that the struggle for control of the ford had been a fierce one. The dead lay in heaps on either side of the river and corpses, half-submerged, still bobbed and floated among the reeds. The crossing was heavily guarded by archers and pikemen wearing the bear and ragged staff of the Earl of Warwick. They told us that they were acting as a corridor to the main English army and urged us to hurry as roving bands of Hainaulters, Philip VI's allies, were still trying to capture the ford and cut off any English stragglers.

On the evening of 24 August we entered the main English camp. We satisfied the commander of the picket line and passed on through lines of foot-soldiers to where the royal pavilions stood. Sir Edmund dismissed the escort and, after a hurried conversation with a royal sergeant-at-arms, escorted me into what I knew to be the royal tent. Flickering cressets revealed a group of nobles dressed in half-armour sitting round a trestle table littered with plates, goblets, and pieces of parchment. They were engaged in furious debate and totally ignored our entrance. I stood there trying to calm my mounting panic by looking at the half-open trunks and caskets, which lay scattered around the tent. Eventually the curtain separating the sleeping quarters from the rest of the tent was pulled aside and the king entered. He was accompanied by Sir John Chandos and a hawk-faced, cold-eyed young man, the eldest son of Edward III's brood, the Prince of Wales. They too were dressed in half-armour and I realized the whole camp must be on a war footing, expecting the French to attack at any moment. The king studied me for a moment before turning to his nobles.

"My lords," he announced, "my scouts have repeated that the French have left Abbeville and mean to bring us to battle." He silenced the rising clamour with a gesture. "We are in a strong position," he continued. "You have your orders – I beg you to retire and inform your marshals." The nobles rose, bowed to the king and trooped out of the tent led by the king's principal commanders, the Earls of Warwick, Oxford and Northampton. I recognized these by the devices emblazoned across their breast-plates. At a sign from the king, Sir Edmund also left with a brief nod towards me and a look which almost mounted to pity. I stood there, too exhausted to speculate on the future.

The king, Chandos and the prince seated themselves on overturned trunks. Chandos and the prince conferred quietly with one another while Edward smiled coldly at me.

"Well, Master Clerk," he rasped, "your report."

I cleared my throat and gave a conventional account of my work so far, omitting any reference to my correspondence with Tweng, my work at Gloucester and, of course, my burglary of the secret seal records. The king heard me out, looked at me quizzically and then shouted, "Guard!"

I really did begin to tremble, wondering if a full confession or a plea for mercy would help. The tent flap was opened but the king simply informed the guard to summon the prince's tutor, Sir William Harcourt. The latter must have been waiting outside, as he had pushed his bulk into the tent before I had time to compose either a question or a plea. He was a balding, bland-faced, stout man, but his reputation as a strategist and warrior belied his grossness. He made an ideal tutor and bodyguard for the prince.

"Sir William," the king barked affectionately, "may I present Edmund Beche, a deserter. In the coming battle, you and my son are to lead the vanguard. I want this coward put in the forefront of that vanguard. Do you understand? Then take him away."

Before I could protest, Sir William's iron grasp shoved me out of the tent. I turned to explain but Sir William's look of contempt killed any hope of being understood. He led me back through the lines up to the top of the ridge where companies of archers were lounging around camp-fires, eating, praying or joking, according to their whim. Sir William told them to watch me and stamped away. After a while, he returned with a conical helmet, a quiver of arrows, a long yew bow and a jacket of boiled leather, together with a belt and a sharp stabbing sword.

"Master Coward," he said, "wear these. If the French attack tomorrow, you will be one of the first to see them. If you die, good riddance, but if you live, then one of these master bowmen has orders to kill you." He began to walk away but then turned back. "Oh, Master Coward," he added, "the same bowman has archers to watch you with orders to kill you if you try to desert again. Even if you do, the French are all over the place and they're taking no prisoners." He looked at me, shrugged philosophically and waddled back down the ridge towards the main camp.

My arrival had caused little stir among the archers; dressed in dusty travelling clothes, I looked little different from them. Once I had fitted on both jacket and belt and gathered up the rest of my armour, I virtually became one of them. I felt too sick to join any group and slumped wearily to the ground, not caring to search out my would-be assassin. He could have been any one of the countless archers surrounding me. I huddled in my cloak, tired and angry at being so cleverly tricked by the king. If Edward had executed me or had me secretly murdered, questions might have been asked, but now my death could be easily explained. To my friends (even to you, Richard), I would appear a brave man who had been caught up with the king at Crécy, volunteered to fight in the front line where, unfortunately, I was killed. On the other hand, to men like Harcourt, I was just another coward going to meet his just reward. I realized that there was little hope for me. I had

served in campaigns before and, like all Londoners, I had
obeyed the statute which laid down that every able man was
to practise regularly with the bow. Nevertheless, if the great
French army decided to spare me, then the unknown master
bowman would carry out his orders. How I escaped my
expected death is a miracle and the reason for this detailed
letter.

At dawn, the camp was roused. I got up, refreshed after a
few hours sleep, collected my weapons and ambled towards
one of the communal cooking-pots for a lump of black
bread, a bowl of messy oatmeal and a cup of watered ale. A
slight mist hung over the dew-wet grass and we had to
breakfast under cloudly skies. The common opinion was
that it would rain and the French would hardly attack. The
marshals ignored such prophecies and began to order us
into lines, so we moved over the ridge and half-way down
the hill. A period of utter chaos reigned and after a great
deal of shuffling backwards and forwards I realized that the
archers had been formed into a series of hollow edges of
arrow-head formations across the muddy hillside. It was a
sound tactic. It presented as small a front as possible to the
enemy, who would break on the point of the wedge, only to
leave his flanks exposed to a hail of arrows, as he was driven
on to the lines of the waiting men-at-arms.

As the morning progressed, Edward's tactics became
more evident. We were divided into three divisions or
battles. The right (in which I was standing) was the farthest
down the slope under the Prince of Wales, and had its flank
protected by a river and the village of Crécy. The division on
the left under the banner of the Earl of Northampton was
further up the slope, its flank being protected only by a
small hamlet called Wadicourt. The centre division was
mainly made up of lines of men-at-arms, who stood on
terraces or cultivated strips, which would impede any

cavalry which survived both the steep ride up the hill as well as the steady hail of arrows from the archers on each flank. Behind the centre at the top of the hill stood the reserve under the king himself. Banners were displayed, flapped brilliantly, and then furled again because of the light drizzle. Trumpets blared and shrilled at each other, stirring the large war-horses and exciting the men. Throughout the morning, the royal broad blue and gold banner flapped near a small windmill which was Edward's central command point. This piece of information was given to me by the archer standing alongside me, a small wiry man with close-cropped hair and a skin burnt brown by the sun. In a thick northern burr, he introduced himself as John Hemple from Pontefract. As I was "green in matters of war" (so he put it), Hemple showed me how to dig a hole in the ground for my arrows and gave a never-ending commentary of the king's strategy. He pointed out that the most interesting feature was that the knights would be fighting on foot, as they had before at Dupplin Moor against the Scots, as well as at the recent battle of Morlaix.

His endless chatter was brought to an end by a roar of approval which spread across the lines as the king, riding a white palfrey, passed slowly along the whole line of battle, stopping now and again to give some encouragement to the troops. As he passed our section, I lowered my eyes, heartily wishing I had the means to plant an arrow firmly in his back.

After the king's review, the marshals ordered us to stand down but to remain in our positions. Food and water were brought along the lines and the archers whiled away their time by throwing dice, trying to sleep, or in endless speculation about the whereabouts of the French. Midday passed and still no news arrived. I sat on a hassock of grass talking to Hemple and other archers, or gazing into the distance wondering how I could extricate myself from the trap in which I found myself. As the day wore on, my anxiety about my personal safety diminished as speculation mounted amongst the troops about whether the French would appear before nightfall. The day had started threatening and a sudden thunderstorm late in the afternoon ended our chatter and cooled our ardour. We rushed to protect our precious bowstrings. Each man unstrung his bow, coiled up the bowstring and placed it inside his cap.

The storm was soon over. The clouds dispersed and we were beginning to shed wet leggings when a series of trumpet blasts made us all turn to the windmill. We could see figures scurrying to and fro, and then one of the archers started shouting and pointing down the valley where the road to Marcheville emerged from the wood. I looked. At first I could see nothing, but then the early evening sun caught the gleam of armour. The French had arrived. Our marshals shouted at us to take up our positions. We stood to arms and watched as the French army, division after division, debouched from the wood and began to advance across the floor of the valley. It was a splendid, terrifying sight. The chivalry from half the courts of Europe were advancing against us, banners and pennants snapping in the evening breeze. Hemple pointed out the great blue flag of France adorned with the fleur-de-lis and, alongside it, the scarlet Oriflame banner. Hemple spat when he saw it and explained that the Oriflame was only flown when the French intended to take no prisoners. It was a sobering thought and I couldn't help shivering when Hemple pointed out that the English force only amounted to about thirteen thousand men, whilst the French must have been more than three times that number.

By now, we archers were ready, arrows notched. We waited for orders as the French milled and turned in glorious colour in the valley.

"The fools!" Hemple muttered. "They're going to attack without waiting to deploy."

In fact, the French did pause to send forward their Genoese crossbowmen, who advanced steadily forward, leaping and shouting till they were within range. Then they stopped, wound up their windlasses and fired an erratic shower of arrows, which drew nothing except derisory catcalls from the lines of waiting English archers. Then our marshals shouted their orders.

"Aim."

"Steady."

"Loose."

The air hummed with our shafts, which darkened the sky like clouds scudding across its surface, before falling with deadly accuracy amongst the Genoese. We never waited to see the effect of our volley for time and again we were ordered to loose until an order rang out ordering us to stop. When I looked down the slope I saw the Genoese lying in thick groups in the grass, many of them hit two or three times by our shafts. the rest were running back to the protection of the French horses, but these simply ran them down as they began their ponderous climb up the hill.

Once again we were ordered to steady, then loose, and, although the French knights were heavily armoured, our arrows had the same deadly effect. Many of the French did make our lines, only to be hacked down, or have their horses killed under them. They were joined by fresh waves who trampled down their countrymen to get at us. The most frightening thing was their terrible anonymity. Great steel-encased figures. Visors down. They rode at us on horses like phantoms from a nightmare. They hacked and whirled sword and mace as they tried to reach us through the wooden stakes. Their great war-horses reared and snorted, flailing sharpened hooves, more wicked than any sword. Many were impaled on the stakes but more and more were getting through.

Soon our front line was heavily engaged in hand-to-hand fighting, while our colleagues at the back poured volley after volley over our heads into the massed French knights. The evening air was filled with curses, shouts and the screams of dying men and horses. At close quarters, my bow became useless. I drew my stabbing knife, dodged sharpened hooves and hacked and clawed at anything which came near me. A French knight loomed over me but I ducked under the belly of his horse, drove my knife upwards and then jumped sideways as horse and rider crashed to the ground. The knight lay thrashing like a baby on the ground but, terrified of being cut off, I hurried back to the protection of my own lines. The situation was now becoming desperate. We had run out of arrows and, though the French were impeded by the weight of their armour as well as their dead, who clogged the ground and turned it a muddy red, it was obvious that they were going to break through our flank by sheer weight of numbers. In fact, the line was beginning to sway and buckle in the centre. Then Edward detached troops from the left flank and sent them to our help. At the same time, he brought up the reserve and the French were forced to retreat.

The sun was now setting but the dying daylight revealed the magnitude of the French losses. The slope was carpeted with dead or dying knights, their colours sadly tarnished, while some of their great war-horses still stood pathetically beside them. We were ordered to recover as many shafts as possible and we surged forward, plucking arrows from the dead and so finishing off those wounded too badly to be taken prisoner for ransom. The marshals put a stop to any plundering and we were ordered to reform and await a fresh attack. I joined my comrade, Hemple, who, talkative as ever, vowed he must have slain a score of French knights. I wondered if the enemy would retreat, but he laughed and pointed downhill where the French assault was reforming. Up they came again, not so quickly as before, but quite prepared to trample their dead to break our lines. Once again they were met with deadly volleys of arrows before they closed with us once more. This time the full English force was committed. The front line, a mixed collection of knights and men-at-arms, held them while the archers shot over their heads. It was soon dark, but a clear night helped our archers, who had simply to aim at the French mass, confident that every arrow found its mark. It soon became apparent that the French had suffered a disastrous defeat and that it was only a matter of time before they conceded the day. Eventually, a series of trumpet blasts, repeated time and time again, ordered the French to break off. As they did so, one knight, maddened by defeat, turned his horse round and rode full tilt at our group. It was an unexpected move and caught Hemple too far forward. The knight sliced at him with his sword, striking at the archer's shoulder, and was turning round for a second charge when I ran forward, knelt and loosed a shaft which did little damage except bring the Frenchman to his senses. He checked his horse, threw down his sword and cantered off into the darkness.

The marshals were shouting at us not to pursue the enemy as I ran forward to Hemple, who was lying face-down in the red mud. When I turned him over, I noticed his shoulder was bleeding badly though he was not in mortal danger. I ripped the cloak off a corpse and tore it into strips and, after cleaning the wound with some wine from my leather bottle, I bound his shoulder as securely as possible. Apart from the chilling moans of the dying, the fighting had now died out. The English lines had drawn back towards the torch at the ridge and the French had retreated into the darkness. I forced some wine between Hemple's lips; he stirred, opened his eyes and looked at me.

"You drove him off?" he asked weakly.

I nodded and told him to keep quiet. He smiled and fumbled at his belt, then I felt his dagger point pressing against my stomach. I looked down at him. "So, you're the master bowman?"

"Yes," he sighed, "with orders to kill you. They said you were a coward." He let the knife drop. "Whoever or whatever you are, you're no coward and I owe you my life. So take my advice. Change clothes with a dead man and go. Now! They'll soon be combing the battlefield for the wounded and will find me. So go! Go!"

I pressed his hand and moved off. I soon found a suitable corpse. He was my stature and his face was badly scarred and mauled. I changed garments and left enough evidence to suggest (at least for a while) that the corpse was that of Edmund Beche. I kept my purse and wallet carrying the royal warrants, then I moved off to seize one of the many horses still wandering the battle-field. I managed to capture a mount, a magnificent brute, but dull with exhaustion, and I then rode slowly north towards the river. My intention was to skirt the English camp and then follow the Somme north till I reached the port of Crotoy. I calculated that the countryside would be denuded of both French and English troops, and this proved to be correct. The news of Crécy had reached the port – God knows how – when I reached it safe but exhausted late the following evening. I sold the horse for a nominal sum and, using the king's warrants, managed to secure passage on an English supply boat plying between Crotoy and the port of London. I spent most of the voyage sleeping for three days in a rat-infested hold, until we docked at the steel-yard this morning. London is celebrating the carnage at Crécy but I know it will only be a matter of time before the king discovers my escape. Therefore I must prepare the resumption of my quest and journey immediately to Italy.

I have written this letter in haste from London. God keep you, Richard. 4 September, 1346.

Letter Ten

Edmund Beche to Richard Bliton, greetings. The day I finished my last letter to you marked the end of my mission in England. I spent that day touring the docks along the river Thames and eventually secured a passage to Genoa on board the *Bianca,* a home-bound cog from that city. I thought it would be too dangerous and too slow to travel overland to Rome, and the Genoese ship seemed to be the safest prospect. It had delivered its spices at the steelyards and its holds were now crammed full with English felts and hides bound for the markets of northern Italy. Moreover, she was part of a well-armed convoy, a small fleet in itself. The master of the *Bianca,* who had agreed to take me (and my English marks), explained that the sea was a constant battlefield. From Land's End to Gibraltar prowled the ships of France, Spain, England, as well as those of Hainault, Holland and the Hanse. Nor was the Middle Sea any safer for it was the hunting-ground of fierce corsairs from the Moorish states of North Africa.

The *Bianca* slipped its moorings two days after I embarked. I was unable to bring my horse, so I sold it and only took my sword, dagger and saddle-bags, filled with a few clothings and all my marks and other different coins I could gather. My lack of baggage proved an asset, for within a week we were battling through the savage winds which lashed the Bay of Biscay into a frenzy, and the master had to jettison all unnecessary cargo. His warnings about the sea-wolves proved to be more than justified. Time and again sails appeared on the horizon but, seeing our strength (it was a convoy of forty ships), none dared draw any nearer. At length the winds dropped and the weather grew warmer as we slipped through the Straits of Gibraltar and came into the Middle Sea. Here, the *Bianca* huddled close with the rest of the squadron. The master explained that the Moorish corsairs attacked in ships driven by long sweeps manned by slaves. They would follow the convoys, waiting for any hapless ship to be left behind and then swoop down on it, like a falcon to the kill. Two days later, in the middle of the day, three long, narrow vessels appeared over the horizon. They lay low in the water, dark sails flapping whilst their oars slowly dipped in the calm, blue sea. They never attacked, for our escort ships spread as a shield, but they kept close and their drumbeats could be heard clear across the water. The master prayed for good winds, explaining that if we were becalmed then the pirates would attack. The wind, however, never dropped and at night each ship lit beacons to prevent a sudden attack through the darkness. For days the corsairs tracked us like starving wolves would a deer but, when we changed tack for port, they gave up the hunt and vanished the night before we entered Genoa.

I would have liked to have visited that city, but time was passing and I stayed in the harbour until I secured passage along the coast to the Roman port of Ostia. I ended up bribing a fisherman, who took my money and then insisted on leaving immediately. His boat looked as old as the Middle Sea itself but it served its purpose and within a week I was in Ostia and on to the old Appian Way to Rome.

Rome might be eternal, but so is its heat, filth, mangy cats and quarrelling nobles. The master of the *Bianca* had warned me to take care and I took his advice to heart. If the Holy City had forced the Pope himself to flee to Avignon, then it was no place for a lonely, English clerk. I avoided the inns and housed with the Franciscans in their monastery on the Travestere. From its tower, I could see the ruins of the Circus Maximus, as well as the vague outlines of what used to be the Forum. After a few days rest, I crossed the Pons Emilius (or the Ponte Rotte according to the plebs) intent on a little sight-seeing. The brothers kindly left me a guidebook, a battered copy of the *Mirabilia Orbis Romae,* but I was disappointed to find most of the ancient buildings covered in rubble which the city fathers refused to clear. The modern quarter only consisted of spacious villas of the ever-quarrelling barons and the yellow tenements which housed the rest of the city's thirty thousand population. Due to the heat and filth in our glorious centre of Christendom, I soon gave up sightseeing and turned to the business in hand. A few inquiries amongst the Franciscans sent me to the Via Lata, where I commissioned a common scribe to draw up the names of all monasteries within a sixty-mile radius of Rome. Then my pigrimage began. I visited every monastery, abbey and convent. Sometimes I was away days but, as the weeks passed, I failed to find any trace of the *Inglese* I was searching for. Scots, Irish, men from Yorkshire and Devon, were there, but after a few questions I dismissed each of them. The search was gruelling and dangerous. Such men had their reasons for hiding from the world, and time and again I was warned off with threats and curses.

One of them, Roger Harnett, became friendly with me. He was an exile from England. In actual fact, an outlaw who had been sentenced to permanent exile by the assizes. He was a thief but one with some charm, and he gaily regaled me with his past history. How he had been apprehended in the New Forest and sentenced at the Winchester Assizes. He had been commanded to walk from Winchester gaol to the coast to seek transport abroad. He had walked for days, always keeping to the highway, and safe as long as he never left it or dropped the small cross he was obliged to carry. At Southampton, through a mixture of bribery and cajolery, he secured passage on a Venetian galley, which took him to Venice. He then travelled south to Rome. That had been five years ago and Roger had survived through casual employment and nimble wits. He knew a great deal about the English exiles in Rome. I exhausted him with my questions but learnt nothing. He never asked the reason for my interrogation; he seemed more than content with my company and attention.

I was coming to the end of my stay in Rome when late one afternoon I joined Harnett in a tavern near one of the city gates, the heat was always intense and the dark coolness of the tavern was a constant refuge despite its dirt, rancid smell and myriad horde of flies and cats. It was also frequented by sailors from every nation and so my English tongue and attempts at broken Italian went unnoticed. Harnett, as usual, was in the corner watching the door. He watched me come in and then languidly waved me to a seat. He snapped his fingers and rattled off an order to a greasy slattern, who slammed two cups of wine on to the table and then grabbed the coins I offered. Harnett watched her move away and then leaned across.

"Do not turn round, but you are being followed."

Naturally I turned immediately and noticed that a small fat man had followed me in. He was balding and red-faced with the impish look of a wizened monkey. He seemed unperturbed by my glare and stared coolly at me. I turned back to Harnett.

"How did you know?" I asked.

Harnett shrugged. "I have noticed him on the last two

occasions." He tapped the side of his pock-marked nose and said, "Be careful! Be careful!"

I shrugged and went back to my drink. I knew that Edward III could not possibly have found my trail. Moreover, the man did not look English and seemed to pose no threat. I decided to ignore him for the while and wait for the evening to cool by listening to Harnett's chatter. The bells of a nearby church were tolling for evening prayer when Harnett and I rose unsteadily to our feet and left the tavern. The stranger had gone and I wondered if he had only been the result of Harnett's suspicious imagination. I remember that the evening air was cool and welcome despite the fetid smells of the alley-way. Harnett was singing some song, a lullaby from pleasanter days. He was still singing when the attack came. Three men came from the shadows and poor Harnett seemed just to walk on to the thin long stiletto of their leader. The attack cleared my head and I drew my own dagger thinking these were Edward's men, but the way they searched for Harnett's purse made me realize that they were bandits, the scum of Rome. Nevertheless, they were just as dangerous as any professional assassins and equally frightening. They were dressed in gaily coloured rags with dark, gaunt, unshaven faces. Once they had searched Harnett, they came towards me. I could have fled, but the moment passed, and I was left with my back pressed against the wine-stained alley wall. Their approach was so relaxed that I thought I was dreaming. They did not even change expression as I adopted a fighting stance. Then suddenly, one of them clutched his chest and stared unbelievingly at the cross-bow quarrel which quivered there. He crumpled to the ground. His two companions stared wildly round and then turned to run. In the darkness behind me I heard a click and then saw both thieves brought short in their escape, arms wide out as they slipped to the ground with two more cross-bow quarrels embedded deep between their shoulders.

I turned and peered through the darkness of the alley-way, looking for the source of my rescue. Then suddenly, the small fat man was beside me. He seemed so calm, his head slightly to one side as he looked quizzically at me. Behind him, I could see three other shadowy figures each armed with a squat crossbow. My rescuer smiled and took my dagger from my grip as if I was some naughty child.

"You were lucky, Monsieur." The man's voice was deep and pleasant. Despite his good English, I realized that my rescuer was French. I wiped the sweat from my hands and muttered thanks. The man shrugged.

"I am sorry that we could not save your friend, Master Beche, but," he smiled, "we saved you. Come." He almost snapped his fingers at me and then turned away. I realized that I had no option but to obey and we left poor Harnett and his murderers in the stinking alley as we made our way back into the city. We walked quickly, the small fat man in front while his three shadowy companions ensured that I followed. We must have walked for miles through a maze of streets which eventually led to a piece of wasteland covered with the ruins of some ancient temple. My guide kept on walking to a group of large stones. He then sat, gestured to me to do likewise, and then stared at me as he mopped his brow and drank from a wineskin he suddenly produced from his cloak. Behind me I heard his companions settle themselves. I remembered the fate of the three thieves and decided to sit as quietly as possible. The silence was eerie, broken only by the wine gurgling in the fat man's throat and the far-off hoot of an owl hunting its prey under a clear Roman sky. Eventually, the fat man belched and passed the wineskin to me. I drank gratefully and realized that the wine was good, not the vinegar of a Roman tavern.

The fat man smiled and leaned towards me.

"You," he said, "are Master Beche, a clerk of the English royal Chancery, and I am Master Jean Raspale, clerk of the French royal Chancery."

He seemed to find the coincidence amusing.

"I am correct, am I not?"

"Yes," I replied. "You are correct."

"Good. Then tell me as one professional to another. Have you found him?"

I stared back at him with feigned innocence.

"Found whom? I am an English clerk on royal business."

Master Raspale cut me short with a laugh and a shake of his head.

"Master Beche, we have established that you are a clerk but not on royal business, otherwise why should your king want you dead?"

I stood up protesting but Raspale curtly ordered me to sit, and then he passed a thin yellowing roll of parchment towards me which he had pulled from his wallet. I opened it and read my own death warrant. It was from the king and dated three days after Crécy and it declared me 'Wolfshead,' an outlaw to be killed on sight for a suitable reward from a grateful king.

Raspale watched me steadily as I carefully rerolled the parchment and handed it back to him.

"Well, Monsieur?" he murmured.

I shrugged. "Even clerks make mistakes."

Master Raspale got up and put his hands on my shoulders.

"Monsieur, you owe me a life."

"I never asked for your help."

"No, but you got it," the little Frenchman replied. "Moreover, you do not have to tell us much. We too have our spies. We know that you are investigating the death, or should I say disappearance, of Edward II."

I looked at him sharply.

"As I have said, we also have our spies. We have known about it for some time, just as we know about the Fieschi letter. So, have you found him?"

I shook my head.

"Do you know where he is?"

"No," I replied. "and, if I did, how would it benefit you?"

Raspale slumped back on his seat. "Edward III has claimed the crown of France. He has ravaged the country and just recently destroyed an entire French army. Anything we can use against him we will. Who knows," he said in a half-whisper, "what we could find? Our spies knew you had sailed to Italy. It was only a matter of time before we picked up your trail here."

"Do you expect me to find Edward II for you?" I asked.

"No, just find him and we will be behind you. We have confidence in you," he smiled. "We can wait."

"And the English king's men?"

"Let us hope that we can complete our business before they arrive."

"I want to complete this mission myself," I replied.

Raspale rose and handed back my dagger. "Do what you have to, Englishman, but we shall be there."

Raspale looked into the darkness and then suddenly turned. "Come," he snapped, "follow me."

I had little choice. I wrapped my heavy cloak round me and followed him into the night. Behind me, padding like faithful mastiffs, came his three companions. Raspale, despite his size and bulk, was a rapid walker. I followed him down a maze of stinking streets. Cats, black against the poor light, snarled and vanished hunting their elusive quarry, still we walked, Raspale slightly in front and his small retinue guiding me before them. We crossed small plazas and entered the more salubrious area of the city. Pilgrims, pimps and prostitutes began to jostle us as we threaded our path through them past busy churches and even busier taverns. At the corner of one plaza Raspale paused, his hand raised as if to give us a warning. I stopped behind him and gazed across the square towards a tavern entrance with torches blazing above the sleek horses tied there and men, heavily muffled against the cool of the night, moving to and fro. Then in an instant, one figure detached itself from the crowd and stood in the pool of light thrown by the flickering cressets. Under the long blond hair, I recognized the gaunt hawk features of Chandos. I could not believe it. He was here in Rome! I turned to see Raspale studying me, his head slightly cocked to one side like an inquisitive robin.

"Well, Monsieur?"

I looked at him.

"Chandos has been here for a few days," he whispered, following me deeper into the shadows.

"How did you know?" I asked.

Raspale shrugged and looked across at the tavern entrance, now deserted except for the restless horses.

"We know, Master Beche," he replied. "We also know that he has been tracking you. We also know that he is going to kill you." He nodded towards the tavern.

"You owe me your life, Master Beche. Twice. Once in the alley and now this."

I looked at him.

"If we had not found you," he continued, "they would have."

I gazed into his dark liquid eyes and I realized that he was speaking the truth.

"I thank you, Monsieur, but ..."

"But nothing Mosieur. We wish to know things. And," he

tapped his nose, "we can tell you something." I nodded my agreement and Raspale seemed pleased with this.

"Be at the tavern tomorrow, Monsieur." He then nodded at his companions. "They will see you home."

So they did, Richard. Through the maze of streets back to the Franciscan monastery. They evidently knew where I was staying – but what really concerns me is how did Chandos learn where I was going – and learn so quickly? This thought still concerns and worries me. I must end this letter. Written in haste from Rome. October 1346.

Letter Eleven

Edmund Beche to Richard Bliton, greetings. The day after I sent the last letter to you proved to be momentous. Let me first explain, I do apologize for the length of this letter, but I did say I would tell you all I know. Moreover, like any good clerk, I find it easy to solve a problem. Once I have transcribed it.

Early in the morning I was to meet Raspale, I awoke, washed and, after eating the bread and grapes supplied by the little brothers, made my way down to the tavern. It was strange to enter its tangy, bitter-sweet atmosphere so early in the day and to find Raspale already there. He looked pert and fresh as if the previous evening's exertions had no effect on him. He sat at his ease behind a corner table, on one side of which lay a small vellum scroll and on the other a cup of wine and the remains of his breakfast. Raspale smiled a greeting, waved me to sit down and called for more wine and a bowl of fruit. He waited until they had been brought before speaking.

"Monsieur, you owe me your life on two counts. So, I think there is a debt to be paid. I have too much respect for you to think I can get it by torture or any other foul means but, as I said last evening, we know a great deal about your mission and for whom you are looking."

"Why?" I asked. "Why is it so important to you?"

131

Raspale shrugged nonchalantly and twirled the cup in his hand, watching the wine twist and turn.

"I have already explained that," he answered. "It does not affect you, and it is a matter of deep concern to my masters." He put the cup down and gazed at me.

"Anyway, why should it concern you? You have no love for your master, King Edward III."

I nodded in agreement, although I was quick to notice that Raspale had almost omitted the word "King." However, I let that pass, as a simple reaction of a French clerk who has seen his country plundered by English armies.

"What can I tell you?" I asked.

"As much as you know," Raspale answered.

He looked beyond me at the ceiling.

"Time is short, Monsieur. I would appreciate a quick summary of what you have found."

I thought for a while. There was nothing to lose. Raspale seemed an honourable man, who had saved my life on two separate occasions. He was right. I owed him a debt and it should be repaid. So I put my arms on the table, leaned forward and began to give him an account of what had happened since that interview so long ago in the chapel at Windsor Castle. Raspale listened intently and, now and again, asked me to repeat certain incidents, placing particular emphasis on Edward III's evident concern for my mission. Of course, I never told him everything. I omitted the fact that I wrote letters to you, and said nothing about Michael the Scot, or Isabella's attempt to kill me. Even so, I was almost hoarse before I ended my story.

Raspale then simply put his wine cup down and stared quietly at me. He then placed his square, stubby fingers on the table and, to my astonishment, asked for my story once again. I protested so loudly that heads in the tavern turned to stare at the corner in which we were sitting.

"Monsieur," Raspale whispered quietly, his face now a few inches away from me. "I want the story again. After all, you do owe me your life and I can be of assistance to you."

He picked up the small scroll which had been lying near him and tapped the table with it. So, once more, I began to recount my adventures and once more Raspale listened attentively, his head slightly cocked to one side as if this helped both his hearing and concentration. After I had finished, Raspale asked me a series of questions. To my surprise, he seemed to concentrate on the Dunheved gang. I told him what I knew about their attempt to free Edward II at Berkeley Castle and of my belief that they probably succeeded, referring once again to the funeral arrangements for the supposedly murdered Edward II. Almost angrily Raspale pushed this aside.

"No, Monsieur," he rapped. "We, or rather I, are much more concerned about Stephen Dunheved's journey to Rome."

For a while I was nonplussed. Then I remembered that in the spring of 1326, a few months before Isabella and Mortimer invaded England, Edward II had sent Stephen Dunheved to the Pope at Avignon. There were rumours that this mission was in connection with Edward II's attempts to gain a divorce from Isabella. I suddenly realized that I had never paid much attention to this. After all, it was a natural reaction of an angry king when he knew that he was being cuckolded. Moreover, nothing had come of it, and I had found no trace of the mission in any of the royal archives. I wryly recollected that an omission of something from the royal archives does not necessarily mean that it was unimportant.

"Why?" I asked Raspale. "Why do you pay so much attention to this mission. Is there something I should know?"

Raspale shrugged and smiled.

"Perhaps, or perhaps not. We shall see."

I stared at him.

"Do you expect me to lead you to Edward II?"

Raspale shook his head.

"No, Monsieur Beche, we follow different paths. But, remember, we shall watch you, and be careful. We do know that Chandos bears orders to kill you outright. Who would care if an English clerk disappeared in the wilds of the Italian countryside? Take care!"

He rose from his stool, tossed the small roll of parchment towards me and quietly swept out of the tavern, his faithful shadows padding behind him.

I decided not to wait any longer myself. I gazed quickly around the room, looking for strange faces or for eyes watching me intently. There were none, but I knew that it was only a matter of time before Chandos discovered where I was and where I drank. I took up Raspale's parchment, leaving the tavern for the last time and made my way quickly back to the monastery. In the solitude of my cell I opened the parchment that Raspale had given me. It was written in Norman French, in a small neat hand, and my heart leapt with excitement when, on a quick perusal, I noticed the word "Dunheved" appearing repeatedly on the first folio. It proved to be a confession and I give it to you word for word.

In the name of the Father, and of the Son, and of the Holy Ghost. I, Peter Crespin, former monk, former conspirator, former friend of the Dunheveds, and one of the last loyal adherents of good Edward II, being of sound mind – though sadly not for long – make my last confession. Soon I will be dead. Neck stretched, tongue out, bowels loose. Yet, what is the use? More to the point, what is the difference between me dead and me living? I was always ready to stretch my neck out, tongue clacking, that is why I am here in a stinking French gaol miles from England and its green grasses and cool rivers. Rouen! What a place to die! And for what? Helping myself to a purse of gold and having to kill a fat merchant for it. I tried to explain to the French notary that I was hungry and that I had not intended to murder. Thank God I told them that I was a former monk. Knowing these bastards they would have probably burnt me. I think it so ironical to be hanged for a theft when the Dunheveds and I plotted treasons so great that we were constantly under sentence of death. When the Dunheveds were broken, I fled England, thinking I would be safe in France. It is so ironical that Death crossed the Channel with me.

I survived on my wits for years but I suppose my luck has just run out. The Dunheveds will turn in their graves laughing and be the first to meet me in Hell. I told the notary I had something to say and I can see that the clerk writing this is becoming impatient because, so far, I have said very little. I am not going to tell all. Why should these bastards, who are going to hang me, know everything I did? I could shake thrones with my knowledge. Stephen Dunheved could have done that, too. He and his clever brother, but they are dead. Isabella, the old bitch, saw to that. Poor sods! They came so near to success, now the grand design is nothing more than their bodies rotting in the ground while I rot in this piss-pot of a gaol.

Time is passing, so I will begin at the beginning. I was born in Hampshire. My parents were free peasants. My father had earned his freedom and then expanded his holding and could boast of twenty bovates of land and an oxen team to till them. His immediate overlord was the Bishop of Winchester, but my father always bragged of his independence. My mother too was proud of their status but was, unfortunately, too wearied to rejoice in it. She bore ten children but only four survived into adulthood. I was the only boy and so my parents doted on me. They spoilt me, gave into me and so I began my long journey both to the priesthood and this gaol.

Let me explain. Although my parents were free and I, too, was free-born, we were still peasants. My father had to work from morning to night. His arms, neck and back developed muscles like a bull and he was almost as coarse as one. He smelt of a mixture of beer, sweat and urine. I can never forget his thick roughened fingers, ingrained with dirt, pushing food into his mouth, which was then swilled down with huge draughts of rude ale. My mother would gaze at him adoringly before turning to me with the admonishment to grow up and be like him. I knew I could never be. I hated the work, the dirt, the grunting of my parents in bed at night, which invariably seemed to leave my mother pregnant. Another little bundle to be wrapped in rags and dumped in a small, simple hole in the graveyard.

But where could I go? A life of military service? I considered it but was sharp enough to realize that it was easy to go but so few came back. While those who did return were cripples who had to live off charity. I recall a group of lads volunteering to be part of the Bishop of Winchester's contribution to Edward I's great force of 1297 against the Scots. I remember watching them go. I ran alongside them admiring their new boiled-leather jackets as they swung down some leafy long-forgotten sunny lane. None came back. They got trapped in some God-forsaken Scottish bog and were slowly slaughtered like a group of dumb oxen.

At first, I never considered the church for our vicar, Father William, was even dirtier and coarser than my father. He could just about mumble a few words of Latin. His sermons were incomprehensible and he was invariably drunk. I always remember a story about my father's going to

see him about the marriage of one of my sisters. Father
William had to consult the blood-book, which records the
blood-line relationships in the village. It is the church's
surety against incest and consanguinity, as well as
guaranteeing that the village's idiot population did not
develop even further. Evidently Father William got the book
down from behind the altar and then sat down to consult it.
My father knelt near him for a while, then, when this
became too protracted, rose and crossed to Father William,
only to find our reverend priest trying to read the book
upside down. My father's shouts of outrage could be hard
the length and breadth of the village. Poor Father William
hid in the church tower for days. My father was a powerful
man with a reputation for an evil temper at the best of times.

No, Holy Mother Church did not attract me. Then, all at
once, matters changed. My father used to make visits to
Winchester, and in the summer of my thirteenth year, he
grandly announced that I could accompany him. It was a
great honour. I had been no further than my village, and
Winchester was as near to me as heaven is now. It was a day I
shall never forget. Even now it cuts like a knife through the
cynicism, disillusionment and tragedy of my life. Winchester, I suppose, is no great marvel, but to me it was the
heavenly Jerusalem that Father William used to babble
about in his sermons. Great stone buildings, cobbled
thoroughfares, columns, colours, and more people than I
ever imagined could exist. Buildings, houses, four storeys
high, ladies in silks with painted haughty faces and their
young men in velvet hose and fur-trimmed capes. Yet it was
the cathedral which fascinated me: long white columns of
stone soaring into the sky and then bending back to give
curved spacious arches. Each arch, each curve told a story or
sung a hymn of praise to its creator. Everywhere the curved
and intricately carved masonry presented the visitor with

scenes of heaven and hell. Naturally, it was the latter with its grotesque half-man, half-beast, population which caught my wandering attention. They presented a world turned upside down; dogs with human faces and humans with the faces of sows, dragons and other beasts I hardly recognized.

My father left me gaping there whilst he went searching for the treasurer's office. I spent those hours in the cathedral, but it was when I wandered into the cloisters that the seeds of my vocation were sown. I remember wandering there in the warm sunshine listening to the bees hum and sing as they plundered the honeysuckle and other wild flowers which grew there in abundance. Leading off from these cloisters were the cells of the monks: clean, whitewashed, comfortable and attractive in their ordered simplicity. The monks, themselves, slipped and padded by me. A few would smile and raise their long white fingers in half a blessing. I envied them. I envied their world, so ordered, so clean, so calm in such beautiful surroundings.

I went back to my village, fully determined to become a monk. Yet I did not tell my parents, as I felt that there was still something missing. My parents, as I have explained, had spoiled me. I was used to being the centre of attention, but if I became a monk then I would lose this. I was attracted by the clean, sophisticated simplicity of their lives, but repelled by the anonymity. I can see the clerk, who is transcribing this, smirk. Of course, I know why the little bastard smirks. My pardon. He knows I had no vocation. Well, let me tell you, I've met few who have. How many of our priests live like Christ? You could count them on one hand.

Anyway, I'm digressing. The clerk has just informed me that he is putting down my oaths and profanities. Good! That's the way I want it. He has also told me, the snivelling little snot, that time is passing and I've told them nothing.

Well, what does it matter? I am going nowhere and I do have something to say. Anyway, at least I'm making sure that one clerk does a decent day's work. It is important for me to tell about my early life, it explains what happens later and reserves my name from the monotonous anonymity of death. My parents would have liked that. Some compensation for all their money and efforts.

To my youth again. I kept my vocation secret as I still had doubts and reservations. Then, one day, a friar came to the village. Not one of your Franciscans, but a Dominican. I had heard vague rumours of these. Clever men, fierce preachers who travelled the countryside preaching God's love and the equality of man. The Dominican who came to our village was no different. Tall, sunburnt, with cropped head and grey-blue eyes, he seemed to tower above us all in his striking black and white robe. He took over our church, ignored the bleatings of Father William and proceeded to deliver sermons to all who would come and, if they didn't, he went looking for them in their homes or working on the great outfields of the bishop. His voice was dark and rich and, with his long fingers curling and twirling, he painted pictures of God and the life hereafter as if he had been there himself. It was a drama which held us spellbound and, when he left, I knew what I wanted to be. A monk, but a Dominican who would hold the stage and yet enjoy the cool, clean solitude of the monastery.

My friend, the clerk, is beginning to mutter, so I'll pass quickly on. Suffice to say that I told my parents. My poor, tired mother was overjoyed, while my father was torn between losing his one and only son and the chance to get rid of what he secretly thought was a cuckoo in his nest. He had daughters and they would provide him with sturdy, industrious grandchildren. There was a great deal of travelling back and forwards to Winchester. Money was exchanged for letters of recommendation and then it was finally settled, I would enter the Dominican house in Oxford.

I left my parents and my village with hardly a backward glance and travelled to Oxford to begin my studies. My dream was realized and, with a few minor exceptions, I was not disappointed. I came to love the clean austerity and regular routine of the monastery, even the religion, for I had a quick brain and a good actor's aptitude for any role. My future as a priest, monk and preacher was assured until I met the Dunheveds, Thomas and Stephen, brothers from a prosperous Gloucestershire family, who had entered the order for the very same reasons as myself. They were like two peas in a pod. Small, dark, intense, with a love of life and a detached cynicism to all around them.

Soon the Dunheveds and I became close friends. Naturally, our superiors frowned on this but, when they discovered there was nothing unnatural or unhealthy about our relationship, the matter was dropped. As I have said, the Dunheveds were as hypocritical as I was. During the day they were regular and committed to their monastic training but, quite often at night I would join them on their forays into the city. The university provided a varied, exciting social life. We drank with the students at the many taverns and, on occasions, even visited some of the brothels near the city gates. So, time passed on. My contacts with my family were seldom and short. Together with the Dunheveds I entered the novitiate, took my vows and was ordained a priest in the summer of 1311. Thomas Dunheved was sent by the order to Wales. Stephen and I, excellent students, were kept at the house in Oxford. Both of us were used to instruct new entrants and to carry out administrative duties of the order. One of these duties was to investigate cases of heresy or schism, these were usually minor matters, hedge priests who had little grasp of theology or some illiterate peasants who claimed they had seen visions of the Holy Ghost.

However, in the summer of 1313 a much more serious matter was brought to the attention of the church authorities. A young student of the University of Oxford, one Simon Palmer, claimed that he was the real son of Edward I and that Edward of Caernarvon was an imposter. He maintained that he had been told all this through a vision whilst walking in Christchurch Meadows. Such impostors were not rare, but this student had a persuasive tongue and was preaching at a time of great political discontent in the country. Edward II was losing the war in Scotland and there was upheaval and unrest following the execution of the King's favourite, Piers Gaveston, by the Earl of Lancaster and others. Edward II had sworn vengeance against his barons and Gaveston's body was still lying in state at King's Langley as Edward refused to allow it to be buried. Even the seasons seemed to conspire against us: a late spring had been followed by a very wet summer. The harvest would be poor and there were other omens and spectres which disturbed the common peace.

Stephen Dunheved and I were instructed to attend the investigation into Palmer's allegations. The Tribunal sat in the refectory of New Hall College with the King's Justices of Oyer and Terminer present, they questioned Palmer whilst we simply sat in as observers. Palmer's story was that years ago at good King Edward I's palace at Woodstock he, Palmer, then the king's first-born, had been playing in the courtyard when he had been attacked by a sow, who had bitten off his left ear. The nurse in charge of him had been so frightened of the old king's temper that she had switched him for a peasant child. Palmer's proof of these allegations was that he bore a passing resemblance to the old king. He also showed us the scar where his left ear had been torn off and, of course, he maintained that his story explained why the present king, in effect a peasant, was so interested in rustic pursuits, such as wrestling, farming and thatching. Dunheved and I wondered whether to laugh or simply advise the royal justices to dismiss Palmer as an idiot. However, the justices were in no mood to treat the matter lightly. They privately informed us that Palmer's allegations were believed by certain members of the court and these charges were bringing the royal name into common disrepute. They concluded that Palmer must be put to torture, even though this was against the law of the land, and the truth ascertained.

A week later the court reconvened, but this time we were informed that the king would be present to watch the proceedings from a gallery. Palmer was brought once more before the justices, and this time he was a different man. He had to be upheld by two sergeants and it was more than evident that he had been tortured. His left eye was closed, his face and neck were covered in bruises, and he had lost the use of his left arm. In a broken voice he confessed that he had been dabbling in black magic and that the devil had promised Palmer that if he proclaimed his story, he would be believed, Edward II would be deposed and Palmer would become the new king of England. The justices asked him in what guise the devil appeared and Dunheved and I had to stifle our laughter when Palmer replied that it had been in the form of a cat. Palmer was then taken back to the cells. The justices were summoned to the royal presence and both Dunheved and I were also ordered to attend.

The king had taken up residence in the infirmary and, when we entered, was standing with his back towards us, studying the one and only tapestry in the room. The justices then knelt before him and we did likewise. The king, however, continued to look at the tapestry and, when I raised my eyes, I thought that he was crying, it was only after a while that I realized that he was shaking with laughter. Eventually he turned and ordered us to rise. My first impression was that Edward II was a king in every aspect. He must have stood over six feet. Long blond hair fell down to his shoulders. His face was long and tanned. His eyes clear blue. He was dressed simply in dark blue robe and hose, with a quilted jerkin over a white cambric shirt. A cloak of the same blue lay thrown across the table, his only ostentation being the large number of rings on each hand, which twinkled and glittered as the king kept nervously stroking his moustache and short fair beard. He looked pleasant and relaxed, though one could detect tension and nervousness as his eyes constantly flickered backwards and forwards. I remembered all the stories about Edward of Caernarvon's being a lover of men. I could not say if they were true, but it was more than evident that men could love him.

He questioned the justices in a low clear voice and then turned to us.

"Well, learned Fathers?" he asked. "What do you think I should do about my brother?"

Dunheved answered immediately that the king's brother was an idiot and should be treated as such. The justices gasped and stood rooted with terror while even I thought that Stephen's impudence would provoke the royal wrath, but Edward simply stared at him for a while and then broke into loud, ringing laughter. He then walked across the room, embraced Dunheved and placed a kiss on each of his cheeks before turning and leaving the room. The justices glared at Dunheved and myself and immediately followed him. The following day we learnt that the justices had had their way as Palmer was to be hanged outside the city walls, although the king's macabre sense of humour prevailed for a cat was also hanged alongside him.

In the following weeks I noticed that Dunheved became quieter, remote and difficult to talk to after our interview with the king. It took me some time to realize that Dunheved had become infatuated with Edward and had fallen under the same spell which had ensnared other men. I remember asking him why he had replied with such impudence, he simply answered that he believed that that was what the king wanted him to do. I could only agree. Edward's presence had been magnetic and even I, cynic as I was, realized that the king was the type of man who either compellingly attracted or totally alienated other people. I could also see that Edward had been attracted, as I had been, by Stephen Dunheved's forthright manner. Consequently, I was not surprised when, six weeks later, Stephen was summoned by the provincial of the order, who informed him that the king had ordered him to be his personal confessor and that he was to join the royal household once it returned from the French court.

Both the Dunheveds and I had now parted company. We kept in touch through frequent letters, but we rarely met and the few times I did encounter Stephen, it was more than obvious that he was a fanatical adherent of the king, the implacable foe of all those who opposed his royal master.

Then, in the winter of 1326 at the height of the crisis between Isabella and Edward II, Stephen Dunheved came to see me. There was a blizzard blowing through Oxford and the city was in virtual hibernation. Stephen simply came to my room, entered without knocking, shrugged off his cowl and sat on a stool near the room's one and only brazier. I let him sit there for a while, hands outstretched, staring into the glowing charcoal. He then turned to me and, even in the poor light, I could see that royal service had aged him. He had that gaunt, passionate look of the fanatic. He was

brusque in his manner and informed me that he had come
to take leave of me as well as receive letters from the Father
Provincial, because he was on an urgent and secret royal
mission to Avignon.

"Why?" I asked.

Stephen pursed his lips.

"It's something terrible. The king wants a divorce."

I pointed out that this was not so surprising in the
circumstances. But Stephen shook his head.

"It's the reasons for the divorce," he whispered.

I urged him to tell me more but he refused and, after
exchanging personal news over a cup of mulled wine, he left
as quietly as he came.

I can see that the clerk who is transcribing this is
beginning to get agitated. Night has fallen, the torches
flicker and he is tired. So I must move quickly to the major
part of my story. Unlike Stephen Dunheved, I did not
become involved in the political disputes between Edward II
and his baronage. I stayed in Oxford as an adviser to the
order and, though not too happy with my life, was content
with the vocation I had chosen. I was a spectator of the
events of 1326 when Isabella, that adultress bitch, returned
from France with her lover Mortimer, and started a
revolution against her husband. Our order was always well
informed and I heard with dismay about the king's rejection
by the Londoners and his consequent flight into the West.

Isabella brought her hordes of mercenaries and exiles to
Oxford. The Mayor of Oxford had to go out to greet her
and I was asked by the Provincial to accompany him to
Woodstock where the queen had taken over the royal
palace. We found the place packed with mercenaries from
the Low Countries and Mortimer's Welsh adherents. The
French bitch received us in the great hall of the palace. She
affected to wear half armour, but even the dimmest member

of our delegation recognized this as simply dress armour intended for ostentatious display. Nevertheless, there was nothing unreal or soft about her attitude. She sat behind a great table at the top of the hall, on her left sat Mortimer, who said nothing but simply stared at us. On her right sat the young prince, and around her the principal captains and advisers of her army. She received the allegiance of the city of Oxford with no more than a nod, demanded the supplies and provender she needed, and pushed a roll of vellum across to our mayor, who by then was almost filling his breeches with fright. The roll was a list of her enemies and included all well-known supporters of Edward II. I noticed with relief that my name was not included but the two Dunheved brothers headed the list. The queen asked me if I knew of their whereabouts. I simply shrugged, made veiled reference to the fact that I was protected by the church and claimed that I had no knowledge of the whereabouts of Stephen or Thomas Dunheved. The queen dismissed my plea with a look of contempt and waved us wearily away.

A day later her army took up pursuit of Edward, who was now fleeing through South Wales with an ever diminishing retinue. I thought of Stephen still in France, and wondered whether Thomas had joined the king in his flight. A few days later the provincial informed me that Thomas had joined the king and had been proclaimed an outlaw. The same edict also ordered the immediate arrest of Stephen Dunheved, if and when he returned to England. We were kept informed of the pursuit of the king and learnt, early in November, of his pathetic arrest at Neath Abbey. Edward, deserted by all, was bound and taken to Kenilworth Castle. I thought of the king I had met a decade ago and felt nothing but pity and compassion at his sudden fall from glory. The Despensers were brutally executed and, for a while, Isabella let the London mob have their way in hunting down and murdering any loyal adherents of Edward II, who were foolish enough to remain in the city. I learnt with relief that Thomas Dunheved had managed to escape his pursuers and knew that he would probably go into hiding in his native county of Gloucestershire, probably in the Forest of Dean, where no royal forces would be able to catch him. I also knew that royal searchers were watching the ports and keeping a vigilant eye on all ships travelling to France with the specific purpose of arresting Stephen Dunheved.

I thought he would never return. Then, one autumn evening in 1327, I returned to my cell after Compline, to find Stephen waiting for me. His eyes looked tired and he had definitely aged, but there was little else to signify that he was an outlaw – almost a 'wolf's-head' to be killed by anyone on sight. We embraced and then he told me that his "business" in Avignon had been shortened by the news of Isabella's invasion and Edward's captivity. He had managed to land in a Northern port, disguised as a seaman, but then travelled south as a Dominican under a false name and on a mythical mission, thanks to a friend in one of the northern Dominican houses. I knew such support would not have been difficult to obtain as Edward II had patronized our order and several of the brothers had been arrested for preaching against the new regime.

I told him to sit down and relax while I went to the refectory for food and wine. When I returned, Stephen was fast asleep on my cot. I let him rest, noticing how the lines on his face had now disappeared. He woke after a few hours, roused by the bells ringing for prime. I did not go down for the dawn service and the ritual chanting which I loved but did not believe in, instead I sat and listened to Stephen's account of how he had crossed the Pennines to meet his brother and others who were now hiding in the Forest of Dean. Stephen's sallow face became flushed with excitement and his eyes glinted with fanatacism. He briefly informed me that Edward II had been moved from Kenilworth to Berkeley, just a few miles from the Forest of Dean, and that he and his brother intended to free the king before the inevitable secret murder of the imprisoned monarch. Cynical as I was, I gasped in horror at what Dunheved had said. I thought of Edward II as I had seen him, tall, regal and vibrant with life.

"They will not kill him," I protested. "He's the king, God's anointed."

Dunheved's abrupt laughter cut me short.

"At Kenilworth," he said, "the king was safe. Henry of Lancaster would see to that, but Berkeley is controlled by Mortimer."

He looked directly at me.

"They will kill him. One way or the other. They will say he died of natural causes or of an accident."

Dunheved silenced my protests with a gesture.

"Kings do have accidents," he replied. "William Rufus had a hunting accident. Rufus' brother, Henry, died at the table and so did John Lackland. Edward II will prove no different."

Dunheved rose and went across to the small slit which served as the only window to my room. He stood listening to the faint chanting, wafted across by the early morning breeze.

"It's a strange task for a monk," he said, almost as if he was thinking aloud.

"It's not what I intended but we all take paths that we never meant to." He paused. "Peter, will you join us?"

Before I could stop myself, I replied.

"Yes, of course. You know I will."

I have often thought why I never even paused. Perhaps it was because I was getting old, tired of the order and of being a hypocrite, of acting a role but never really believing in it. I had realized my dream and found that it was only a dream but, above all, I was bored. I wanted change, something to happen and this was it.

The advantage of being a monk was that my possessions were few. I collected food from the refectory and money from the almoner. Stephen and I then slipped out of Oxford and travelled without mishap to Gloucester. Here I finally discarded my Dominican robe and, after sheltering for a few days at an inn, we made contact with Thomas Dunheved. He simply joined us one morning at the table, acting as if he had always been with us. He had not aged like his brother. He was still the arrogant, cynical, cocky bastard he had been in his student days. He was not surprised to see me but simply smiled, kissed me on both cheeks, and welcomed my support to what he described as the "noble enterprise." He then told us to finish our meal and join him at the horselines.

We left Gloucestershire late in the afternoon and made our way to the fringes of the Forest of Dean. Before I entered, I looked up at the windswept, rain-hanging sky and realized that now, on a wet September afternoon in the year 1327, I was about to become an outlaw. I felt no regrets, only a determination to see the matter through, to release some of the violence pent up during my long monastic career. No sooner had we entered the forest than a guide, who had been expecting us appeared and began to lead us through tortuous ways and tracks to where the Dunheved group had assembled under Sunyat Rocks. These cliffs tower high above the forest and provided us with a view stretching across the trees to the north and the Wye valley to the south. The gang Dunheved had assembled there was a motley collection of outlaws. Scum of both city and forest as well as those few loyal aherents of Edward II, who had either escaped execution or had not fled abroad. They included one or two knights of the shire, a number of Dominicans, and a few members of the household of Edward II or the Despensers. They were determined ruthless men. Many had grievances against Mortimer because of the way he had extended his power in South Wales and along the Welsh March. Most were men from that part who knew the forest well and were totally determined to attack Berkeley and rescue their former king. They did not welcome me and, at first, regarded me with suspicion. However, once they saw the high regard in which I was held by the Dunheved brothers, then they came to accept me as one of the group.

The ballads we often sing about life in the greenwood forest may sound pleasant, but even in the early autumn the reality is very different. We lived in rough shelters, constantly moved camp and attempted to keep fires to a minimum. We depended for supplies on sympathisers from local villages and in the city of Gloucester. We were under no illusion that Mortimer had despatched search parties all along the Welsh March, as well as into the Forest of Dean, hunting out potential sympathizers of the late king. Moreover, there was always danger of traitors in our midst. Of spies who would sell us for a bag of gold or a promise of a free pardon. In fact, one of our group, Matthew Taylor, was tried and hanged by the Dunheveds after it was established that he was in communication with the sheriff of Gloucester and royal officials in the city. I was shocked at Stephen Dunheved's ruthlessness. The proof he produced was not convincing; letters found on Taylor's person which proclaimed throughout Gloucestershire and the rest of the countryside that Dunheved and his gang were traitors. I noticed with a silent shiver that my name too appeared in this proclamation. Taylor attempted to protest but the Dunheveds simply had a rope tied round his neck and three of our company were detailed to take him a few yards to an overhanging oak tree and hang him.

The Dunheveds hardly bothered to wait for his body to stop twitching before they ordered an assembly of all the company and detailed their plans. They pointed out that Isabella and Mortimer were going to be in the north for their projected campaign against the Scots. This would mean that Mortimer would take as many troops as possible north with him. Stephen Dunheved also pointed out that Edward II had been some time in Berkeley Castle and that it was only a matter of time before the former king's death was arranged. He announced that we would be leaving the Forest of Dean in small groups and assemble at the village of Bardby, only a few miles from Berkeley. There we would be joined by other volunteers, who would bring us all the necessary arms and provisions. I remember questioning him on how we were expected to attack a fortified castle, but Stephen simply smiled and said that difficulty had already been overcome.

I was detailed to accompany the Dunheved brothers and, as we travelled north to our assembled point, I tried to question both of them regarding what we should do if we were successful in our venture. I then realized that these two hot-headed fanatics really accepted that Edward, who had been deposed without a blow, would be able to rally tremendous support behind him once he had been freed. I also realized that they had not thought of the political implications of what they were doing. I tried to point out to Stephen that Edward II's son was now crowned king – a beautiful young man accepted by all sections of society. Stephen simply looked at me for a while and then gently reminded me of his mission to the Papacy at Avignon: He told me that he had information and proof which would bring down Isabella, her son, and Mortimer with the greatest of ease. When I pressed him further on this, he simply gave me that strange slight smile and told me to reserve my strength for the journey and the struggle.

I began to wonder what madcap scheme I had so quickly allowed myself to become embroiled in, but I never regretted it. I enjoyed the freedom, the sense of purpose, the military talk of my companions and the desire to achieve something before I died. I reasoned that if I succeeded, then a source of power would be open to us, and if we failed then, remembering Edward as I saw him in Oxford, we had died attempting to achieve something memorable and outstanding. This thought comforted and reassured me.

On 21 September 1327 the Dunheved brothers and the rest of their companions assembled in the forest outside the village of Bardby. None of our companions had been captured, which seemed to prove the Dunheveds' belief that the search parties organized by Mortimer had now been called off because of the Scottish campaign in the north. There were wagons at our meeting points full of arms of every description, helmets, breastplates, jackets and leggings of boiled leather, chain-mail, axes, grappling-irons which must have been taken from fighting ships, as well as bows, crossbows and bundles of long ash-made arrows. When I saw this armoury I realized that the Dunheveds and the captive Edward must still have friends in powerful positions.

On the evening of the same day we moved to Berkeley. The Dunheveds made us go in groups and keep to the forest. We were anxious to avoid any mounted patrols from the castle, yet we encountered none. It was dark by the time we reached the assembly point. Thomas Dunheved divided us into two groups, one would stay with him (I was included) while the other group would go with Stephen. Apart from the two Dunheveds, none of us knew how this second group was to enter Berkeley. We were informed that it was by a secret route, but not given any further description. Thomas was to wait for fire arrows to come from the castle before moving his group up to the walls. Thomas and Stephen drew away from us all, exchanged whispered comments, clasped each other closely and then Stephen called softly to his group and disappeared into the darkness. We whispered our farewells and then crouched quietly listening to the lonely hoot of a hunting owl and the soft crackle of undergrowth as the night life of the forest went hunting or was hunted.

Eventually, Thomas whispered his instructions, and we moved forward as soundlessly as possible. Despite the cool of the night, I found myself sweating, tense, clutching the sword and shield I carried so tightly that the steel rubbed my hand raw. I was terrified and yet exhilarated. The fact that we were now moving intensified the urge to break and run, to be free of that hot crouching line of men following each other into the darkness. A slight rain had fallen earlier in the evening, turning the fallen leaves and bracken into a damp covering underfoot. Once I slipped and fell, the man behind me cursed as I flailed out with the shield strapped to my arm, and for a moment I felt like lying there, my hot face pressed against the cool dark earth. I arose and moved on, conscious only of my thudding heart my sweating body and the figure moving ahead of me. Just when I thought I would be unable to continue, a whispered order told us to stop. I immediately dropped both my sword and shield and lay down. Above me, through the interlaced leaves and branches of the forest I could see the stars as the autumn rain clouds broke up under the quickening breeze. I realized that I was still a peasant's son, anxious about the weather, the clouds and the winds. The next moment I was asleep only to be wakened by Dunheved, who hoarsely whispered me forward. I took my arms and moved up with the rest.

We had reached the edge of the forest. The moon, much to Dunheved's concern, had broken clear out of the clouds, revealing how the ground dropped away to flat marshlands which surrounded the dark mass of Berkeley Castle. My heart sank as I looked at the tall walls, high towers and sealed drawbridge, so distinct in the light of the autumn moon. I wondered how we could cover the ground underneath and then scale those sheer walls. It seemed an impossible task. Nor did the castle garrison look as if it was unwary. I saw the tiny jabs of flares of torches on the battlements and the pinpricks of light through the arrow slits. I whispered my angry objections to Dunheved, but he ignored me and looked at the sky and waited, listening intently to the sounds around us. Once I thought I heard the faint clash of steel on the night air but then dismissed it as a phantom of my fevered imagination. Dunheved sat crouched like some hunting dog, while around us the rest of the group fidgeted and whispered and concentrated on the castle before us. I was wondering what the Father Provincial would think of us now and took pleasure at the prospect of his solemn pomposity's being pricked, when Dunheved suddenly clutched my arm. I looked to where he was pointing and saw the moon slide behind thick, heavy clouds. We waited tense and expectant. Then, one after another, like falling stars, we saw the fire arrows break the darkness above the castle walls.

Dunheved said: "Come, keep to the causeway."

We then clambered down the slope and made our way towards the walls. We had been warned to keep to the causeway and avoid the marshy, swampy ground. One of our company failed to follow this advice and we left him floundering in our mad rush to the walls. I wondered wildly how we were to cross the narrow, stinking moat that our scouts had warned us about. I also noticed that none carried

ladders or grappling hooks for us to clamber the walls. Then
an arrow whipped past my face, another took the man
behind me full in the throat. I turned, but he was already
choking on his own blood. A hand pushed me forward and I
blundered on. I realized that Dunheved was leading us away
from the causeway and the main gate. Ahead of us I saw a
spluttering pitch torch being waved as a signal further along
the wall. I realized that Stephen Dunheved had not only got
into the castle but had seized a postern gate. Arrows still
sliced the darkness and I saw and heard some of my
companions go down. Then we were at the gate. Stephen
Dunheved was there. No longer the Dominican or secret
conspirator but a wild fighting man. His clothes were torn
and his right arm and the sword he held were covered in
blood. He yelled at us and threw the torch up the steps
leading to the battlements. Then the moon broke from its
clouds and behind him, across the castle yard at the foot of
the great keep, we could see a struggling mass of men.
Thomas pushed his brother back towards them and shouted
at us to follow him as he rushed up the steps to the parapet
behind the crenellated castle walls. I did not know what was
happening but later realized the tactics the Dunheveds were
using. Evidently, Stephen's group had launched the surprise
attack, hoping to reach the royal prisoner while Thomas's
group were to attack those members of the garrison still
manning the walls. This would prevent them joining the
group near the keep, as well as spread the impression that
the entire castle was under a major assault. At the time,
however, I could not analyse such military niceties. I was
hot, tired and so terrified that I felt my bowels dissolve like
water. I could die or, even worse, be taken a prisoner.
Terror is a great life-saver and I followed Dunheved up
those steps, determined to live.

The ensuing fight was a bloody struggle. Before we

reached the top of the steps, the enemy was there. Determined men, they soon realized that we blocked the way down and yet, on the narrow, stone walk way, they could not deploy their full force. Instead, they concentrated on pushing us back down the steps. I never really saw them, but I hacked and stabbed at the mass before me. My sword arm grew heavy, and at one time I felt that I could scarcely breathe in that thick struggling mass. Slowly we were pushed back down the blood-slippery steps. Once I looked across to the keep and noticed that the group, much smaller now, were also being pushed back towards us. I felt I could not go on and slipped back into the group of men behind me, allowing another to take my place, and stumbled wearily to the bottom of the steps. A group of companions still stood guard near the postern gate. I looked for Stephen but I was informed that he had been taken wounded back to the forest. I looked back up the steps at the now uneven struggle and wondered how long it could all last. Then I heard the long, haunting sound of the horn coming from the forest, cutting across and, for a moment, silencing the fury of the killing ground. Twice it was repeated, ordering us to fall back, to retreat. I did not wait. Other braver souls may have stayed to guard the postern, our only exit and means of escape but I was through it. I made my way cursing and sobbing to the causeway and I ran, casting away my sword. Behind me I heard others following but, as the fighting in the castle ended, the deadly rain of arrows began again. I heard them whistle and thud and that soft smacking sound as they dropped a screaming man. Soon, I was at the bank climbing up to the same spot from where we launched our attack. I paused, just for a while, then I rose and staggered into the trees. I knew I had to hide before horsemen from the castle began their hunt. I suddenly realized that I was alone, and I wondered where the

Dunheveds were and if they had been successful. Was Edward II free? I found that I did not care. I was tired, bruised, and could only curse the terrible restlessness which had taken me from my village and then my chosen profession to fight to the death alongside fanatics and rebels.

Eventually, cursing myself, the Dunheveds as well as every prince and king, I took shelter in some heavy undergrowth and fell into an uneasy sleep. I woke the next morning cold, bruised and so numb that I wondered whether I could still walk. The morning was sunny and clear, and the song of the forest birds mocked my horrors of the previous night. I listened intently for sounds of pursuit and then crawled from my hiding-place. I ate some dried meat from my pouch, drank and bathed in a small stream. I began to feel better and decided to keep to the forest and return to the assembly point near Bardby before moving back into the Forest of Dean. At first, I found it difficult to walk, but the previous night's sleep and fear of capture kept me going. I saw no sign of pursuers, except a corpse swinging from a tree in a glade that I did not cross but went around. I thought I recognized the body, a member of the Dunheved group, but I dared not approach it. I reasoned that any pursuit from Berkeley Castle may have already swept this part of the forest, or that the local commander may have even concentrated on another area. After two days I was near Bardby and so struck deeper into the forest, searching for the assembly point. Eventually I found it, a small clearing near some overhanging rocks. When I arrived, it looked deserted, then I saw the figure seated, head down as if asleep, against a tree. It was Stephen Dunheved. I looked around and, once satisfied that we were alone, began to move towards him. At once the head snapped up and I stopped when I saw the raised crossbow with its barbed, evil bolt pointing towards me. Stephen's face was white and gaunt, and the eyes were black circles glaring at me. I could see that his right leg was covered in dark crusted blood. I hoped that he was not too feverish to recognize me.

"Stephen," I said. "It's Peter."

Stephen stared, then gave that slow smile and, lowering his crossbow, said, "Peter, are you alone?"

I nodded and he waved me forward. I knelt beside him.

"Stephen," I said, "Is there anything I can do?"

He shook his head. "Did the king escape?" I asked.

Again, he shook his head.

"I don't know," he replied. He paused, grasped his leg and let his head sag forward on to his chest. I thought that he had fainted but then he continued.

"I don't know if the king escaped. I thought I saw a figure being carried towards the gate." He gasped and waited till the pain passed.

"I've seen nobody except you. Perhaps I'll never know." He turned and smiled.

"And you," he continued, "what will you do now?"

"Try and get you to a place of safety," I replied.

Stephen shook his head and pulled a small fat purse of gold from his belt.

"Take this," he said, "and go, now!"

I tried to plead with him, half-heartedly, I admit, for I could see that it was impossible to move him, because of his wounds. Stephen was adamant. I was to leave, and so I prepared to go. However, just before I rose, he grabbed my arm.

"Peter," he said, "let me tell you the secret I took to Avignon." He then pulled me closer and whispered in my ear. I was so astonished that I recoiled in horror and stared speechlessly at him. Stephen then waved his hand at me.

"Go, Peter, now you have the secret which would rock

kingdoms and thrones."

I left him there, alone in the glade, and turned deeper into the forest. I found it difficult to grasp what he had told me but, at the same time, fear and self-preservation made me concentrate on securing my own escape.

To cut this long story short, Master Scribbler, I did escape and came with my "secret to totter kingdoms and thrones" to France. I have had a number of trades but never once acted as a priest. That is behind me. I heard rumours of the capture and death of the Dunheveds, and then the news of Mortimer's fall. I even heard news of Edward II's being alive and free but nothing substantial. However, what I know, I will hold.

So, Master Clerk, stop sitting there on your cold little pink arse and go and tell your masters that I have news that will shake and overturn the throne of England but, in return, I want a pardon and thirty pieces of gold.

This confession was taken from Peter Crespin, a self-confessed murderer and thief, in the town gaol of Rouen in December of the year of Our Lord 1344 by one Henri Tillard, clerk to the king's justices.

Post Scriptum

Edmund Beche to Richard Bliton. This long confession of Peter Crespin seems to hint that my mission has something more to it than finding out what happened to Edward II, or even if he is still alive. It is connected with the mission of Stephen Dunheved and I could curse myself for overlooking that episode. Crespin knew something, he learnt it from Dunheved and it must have bought him his life, otherwise how would Raspale know? I believe that Crespin gave details about his early life to establish his authenticity, and both he and his story must have been accepted by the French

court. This explains Raspale's mission to Italy as well as his
interest solely in Dunheved's mission. The latter is evidently
more important than Edward II's escape? What could it be?
I feel like searching Raspale out and asking him but that
would be too dangerous. God knows. Pray for me.
Rome – October 1346.

Letter Twelve

Edmund Beche to Richard Bliton, greetings. I have found what I have been looking for and, though my mission is at an end, I shall tell you all, rather than cry "finis" and lapse into silence. This letter is the last that I shall ever send you. Indeed, I think I shall never see you again. I am sending this letter in a copy of Aristotle's *Metaphysics*. This is a gift to you, Richard, a token of friendship I shall always cherish.

I awoke early the next morning, determined to get out of Rome as quickly as possible. I intensified my searches, always aware that Raspale might be watching me and that he could well be joined by envoys from England. I felt like the hunter who was quickly becoming the hunted. I decided to ask the Franciscans for aid, and I approached an English friar who had befriended me and lent me the guide book. I swore him to secrecy and vowed that my mission was not immoral or dishonest, but that I needed to leave Rome as quickly and quietly as possible. The friar smiled, padded away and came back with a Franciscan robe.

"Tomorrow," he said, "certain of the brothers are leaving Rome. Put this on and go with them. It would be safer if you camped outside the city."

I did as he said. The following morning I put on the brown coarse robe, paid the brothers for a small sturdy cob and left the eternal city as a bowed, cowled friar. The Roman countryside was a peaceful contrast to the heat and dirt of the city. The red soil, the leafy vineyard terraces and cool olive groves. When I thought it was safe, I dropped to the back of our silent cavalcade and turned quietly into an olive grove. I took off the brown heavy robe and made my way deeper into the grove. I decided to stay near the main highway and resolved to camp in a cave at the foot of some cliffs at the far end of the grove. From there, safe from Raspale, I continued my searches.

I never gave up hope and I was planning to extend my radius even further, when I visited the small monastery of St Albert at Butrio. Butrio is a small, whitewashed village nestling at the foot of a cypress-filled valley. The monastery lies a few miles to the east of the village. It consists of a small chapel, a cloister and a cluster of outbuildings, bounded by a thick, huge wall. I made my way to the main gate and pulled hard at the bell rope. A smiling lay brother, chattering like a magpie, opened the postern door and beckoned me to enter. He never asked my business but, bowing and smiling, led me through the cloisters and into the small, whitewashed cell of the prior. The latter was a plump grey-haired man who sat peering at a manuscript which rested on an intricately carved lectern. When the lay brother announced me, the prior sighed, closed the manuscript and rose to meet me.

"Have you read Boethius, *De Consolatione*?" he queried in perfect Latin. I quoted an extract fluently and his brown face broke into a charming smile. "Good," he exclaimed, "now I know the story about all Englishmen being tail-wearing barbarians is false."

He went across to a table, poured me a goblet of wine and asked how he could help me. I explained, as I had already done a hundred times, that I was looking for an Englishman who, I understood, had retired to a monastery near Rome.

The prior ran his hand through his mop of grey hair and shook his head.

"An *Inglese?* Here? A member of our order?" He shrugged and shook his head. "No, my son, there is no one here from your misty island. Our monastery is comprised of local men."

His gaze wandered back longingly to the lectern and the manuscript that he had left. Then he gasped; "Ah, *mi fili,* of course, I am thinking of the brothers. But there is Hugolino or Hugh, as you would call him. He is not a brother, but he works here as a gardener and a carpenter." He pointed to the lectern. "He carved that. Poor Hugolino, he has been here so long that I almost forgot him." He shrugged in that charming way the Italians have. *"Sic transit memoria mea."*

The name "Hugolino" awoke a dim memory and set my heart thudding with excitement. "May I see him?" I exclaimed. "Of course," the prior replied. "He is attending the flower-beds around the cloisters. I shall take you there."

I hadn't noticed anyone when I passed through the cloisters before, but when the prior took me back, I saw a man, dressed in a brown robe, turning over the soil around a young rosebush.

"May I see him alone?" I asked.

The prior smiled understandingly and padded quietly away. I stepped over the yellowing brick wall and walked softly across the grass, but the man heard me and turned swiftly. He was a thick-built man, about six feet tall with grey,close-cropped hair. His face was dominated by hooded eyes and a nose which curved like the beak of a hawk. I only had the faintest description about Edward II, but something about this man's bearing told me that he was no common gardener. I decided to waste no time and, just before I reached him, I knelt on one knee, bowed my head and murmured, "Edmund Beche, clerk, petitions Edward of

Caernarvon, King of England, Duke of Aquitaine, and Lord of Ireland, for a favour." Only the tinkle of a small fountain broke the silence which followed my salutation. I kept kneeling and was beginning to wonder if I had acted too hastily, when a low, steady voice speaking fluent Norman French ordered me to rise. When I did, I found the gardener sitting on the low cloister wall, gazing speculatively at me.

"Sit down, Master Beche," he said. "Tell me, do you always call common gardeners king and lord?"

I looked directly into his face and noted how the laughter lines crinkled his mouth and pale, blue eyes.

"No, sire," I replied, "only to Edward of Caernarvon, who escaped from Berkeley Castle and confessed as much to Manuel Fieschi at the papal court in Avignon."

At the mention of Fieschi's name, the gardener grimaced and threw down his trowel.

"So," he said meditatively, "the man prattled, broke the seal of confession." He laughed. "Perhaps he didn't, for I told him who I was after absolution. But who are you? Who sent you? The king? My good wife? How many men have you brought with you? I warn you not to harm these good brothers. They do not know who I am, so if I have to die, take me out to do it. After eighteen years, I am more than ready."

I was alarmed at the drift of his speech and, without hesitation, I began to tell him all I knew. He ignored the bell for the midday meal and I talked until my voice was hoarse, whilst he, head bowed, probed at the ground with his trowel.

When I had finished, he rose and extended his hand. "Come, Master Beche," he said, "you have travelled far, talked much, and need refreshment." He led me across the cloisters to one of the outbuildings where he had his cell, a small, clean chamber with a bed, a table and a few stools. He poured me a cup of wine, pushed a basket of fruit into my lap and then sat opposite me on the edge of his small bed.

"Where shall I begin, Master Clerk?" he asked. "Both of us know who I am, but you are wrong on one small count. I am not a king. I was legally deposed and, in the eyes of my former subjects, I have even ceased to exist. All you have told me is true, but I can guess at the question which is still eating away at you. Why have I not returned? Why did I not raise troops to win back my throne, instead of hiding away in a small Italian monastery?" He smiled and swilled the wine around in his cup.

"At first," he explained slowly, "I wanted to do all these things, but once I was free from Berkeley, I also found that I had escaped the hurly-burly of kingship. No one gladly relinquishes his power, Master Beche, but in my case, it is true. My father spent all his life training me to be his heir but when the crown came to me, I found that I not only had to fight the French, the Scots and my own barons to keep it, but live with a woman I grew to hate. It's a high price to pay for any crown, but I was forced to pay more: my only friends, the Despensers, were taken from me and executed. Both did wrong, as I did, but they died simply because they were the king's confidants, and so carried the blame for all his mistakes. My father wanted me to be king, my wife derided me because I did not act like one, and the barons attacked me because I refused to be the kind they wanted. They would have certainly killed me at Berkeley, but Dunheved organized my escape. I never knew how Dunheved managed to enter the castle. I merely heard scuffling, then the flagstone covering the pit was raised, I was dragged up, a bundle was thrust in my hand, and I was led to the postern gate of the castle. My guide managed to get me through but, whilst I was following him out, an arrow took him straight in the neck. Despite my imprisonment, terror forced me to run, and only after a few hours did I stop to rest. I opened the bundle and found a set of clothes, some bread, a knife and a bag of gold. For a while, I waited for Dunheved but, when I could gather no news of his whereabouts, I decided to flee to Ireland. From there, I sailed to France and wandered to Avignon, and from there into Italy. At first I thought that Isabella and Mortimer would instigate a great search for me. But then I heard about their mock funeral and decided that silence was the better part of valour. I was forced to reconsider my position. If I did claim to be king, I would either be dismissed as a fool or executed as a dangerous fanatic. However, the failure of Edmund of Kent's pathetic plot showed that there was little chance or even support for my restoration. On the heels of this decision, came the swift realization that I had no desire to be restored. All I really wanted was peace, and here I have found it." He paused to light two candles before continuing.

"I was not an evil king, Master Beche, but simply a man unfit to be one. My country suffered because of it. My friend, Hugh Despenser, died because of it. That is why I took his name, as an act of reparation." He looked at me beseechingly. "Do you understand?"

"Sire," I began.

"Never call me by that or any other of my titles," he interrupted. "If you do, I shall be forced to ignore you. Well," he smiled, "your question?"

"It concerns the queen dowager," I muttered, "Isabella, your wife."

Hugolino laughed throatily.

"Isabella ceased to be my wife when she opened her legs to another. To be charitable, one must be just, Master Edmund. Isabella was, is, and will probably always be a veritable bitch, a she-wolf. She has never changed and she probably thinks the same about me. So she guards herself against my return. But," he rose, "let the dead rest, and Isabella is dead to me. Come," he smiled, "I'll show you to your quarters and tomorrow you can rest and we can talk again."

Since then, Richard, I have continued to stay at Butrio. I have no desire to return to England to face the vengeance of either the king or Isabella. Nor is there anything there to draw me back. At Butrio, on the other hand, I have found peace. The prior was only too willing to house an Oxford clerk with whom he can debate the finer points of theology, as well as one so proficient in the use and treatment of ancient manuscripts. Hugolino, too, pressed me to stay and we have become constant companions. We discuss every topic under God's heaven, except the English court, a subject he studiously avoids. So, Richard, I shall never return to England. I beg you to destroy all letters I have sent and to keep, as if under the seal of confession, all I have ever told you.

Goodbye. Written at Butrio – 30 November 1346.

Letter Thirteen

Edmund Beche to Richard Bliton. I am sure that you of all people never expected another letter from me, but I want to write to tell what has happened, for you, my dearest of friends, have a right to know. The psalmist was certainly correct when he said, "Nothing lasts under the sun" – not even friendship. Hugolino and I settled down at Butrio, oblivious to the world and with an equally childish belief that the world had become oblivious of us. I was arrogant in my belief that I had evaded and would evade, all my pursuers. I was awakened to the stark reality on the morning of the Feast of the Purification. It was a fair day. The prior and Hugolino had drawn up a list of articles they wanted me to purchase in nearby Butrio. I ambled down to the village on the monastery's one and only donkey and was returning past the Carafe, a small inn, when I distinctly heard a sharp English voice which cut through the hot midday air like a knife. I immediately dismounted and rushed to investigate, but all I found were four, swarthy individuals who answered my inquiries with blank looks, shrugs, and when I pressed them further, a stream of profanities which would have done justice to any denizen of the Roman slums. I began to scour the countryside. All I found were some fresh horse tracks. But whose were they? Innocent pilgrims or my pursuers from the French and English courts? Then early one brilliant morning I found the French. I came up a small hill with an olive grove scattered along the top. I saw some horses grazing aimlessly well away from where the first corpse lay face down in the grass with the garrotte cord still tight around his neck. I hurried forward into the trees. There in a clearing I found Raspale and his group lying as if in sleep, the hempen cords of their assassins wound like necklaces around them. I found a few footprints but it was obvious that Chandos's group had struck probably the night before. They had disposed of the guard and then destroyed Raspale and his group with consummate ease.

I returned perplexed to St Albert's and said nothing, although Hugolino noticed that I was troubled. My fears grew a few days later when the prior bustled anxiously into my cell and reported that the brothers had begun to notice small groups of horsemen which did not hinder them, but kept the monastery under close surveillance. I pacified him, but not my own fear, which pierced my belly with red-hot needles. I went and told Hugolino all I knew. He listened quietly then, putting down the shovel he was holding, announced with great conviction, "They're the English king's men."

"Your son's!" I exclaimed.

Hugolino knelt down on the ground and wiped the soil from his hands.

"No, Edmund, I said they were from the king of England, and not from my son."

I told him that this was not the time to draw distinctions between begetting and disinheritance. He grimaced and asked me to sit alongside him.

"Why, Edmund," he queried, "did the king appoint you to your task? To find me? For what purpose? The people believe that I am dead and, even if I could declare who I am, what difference would it make? The people deposed me and crowned another."

"The French could use you," I interrupted, "as a figurehead against the king."

Hugolino dismissed this with a perfunctory wave of his hand.

"Edmund, Edmund," he asked, "who would believe them? No, I shall tell you why the king has sent you and others to find me. Because, Edmund, he has less claim to govern England than I. Why? Because he is not my son, but the bastard offspring of Isabella and Roger Mortimer."

Hugolino stopped my rush of questions with a gesture before continuing.

"I was never sure of the relationship between Isabella and Mortimer until she joined him in France. I began to make inquiries, yes, I even used torture to get to the truth. By questioning members of her household, I found out that Isabella's relationship with Mortimer dated back years and began during the summer of 1311 while I was in the north. When I learnt of her pregnancy, I was surprised, but the thought of adultery never entered my mind. We'd had intercourse on a few occasions and so conception of a child was not impossible. Only in 1326, whenIsabella was abroad, did I find out the truth and I was too proud to proclaim myself a cuckold for the amusement of the rest of Europe.

"How did the present king get to know?" I asked.

Hugolino smiled mirthlessly.

"Just before he went to join his mother in France, I told him. I screamed his bastardy at him and told him to go. I believe Mortimer knew and taunted him with the fact. That's the real reason behind the coup which overthrew Mortimer and sent him gagged to his death. Now, Edmund, can't you understand why the king wants me? He believed me dead, whatever the circumstances. When he heard from Fieschi that I was still alive, then he had to track me down. Can't you see, Edmund, the king has plunged all of Europe into war for the crown of France, yet he hasn't even a claim to the one he wears. No bastard issue can ever inherit the English throne. He is frightened that I shall open my mouth and disown him before all Europe. Even if I was dismissed as an idiot, the rumour I would start could do him more damage than any threat the King of France could ever pose. It is that information which Dunheved took to Rome, which he later passed on to Crespin. Once the French court learnt about it, then it was only a matter of time before they too started their hunt."

Hugolino stopped and looked at me.

"Master Clerk, the king may not be my son, but he is Isabella's, and possesses her ruthlessness. My friend, whether you like it or not, we are both dead men."

He rose, touched me lightly on the shoulder and walked back to his cell.

I shall not tell you how the rest of that day passed. But I did decide that I could not sit and wait to be slaughtered like some dumb ox. The next morning I armed myself and set out to explore every nook and cranny of the entire valley. Five days I searched. I found nothing, although I suspected that I was being followed and watched at every step I took. Eventually, I turned my tired nag back to St Albert's. I was aware of its great bell tolling slowly, long before it dawned on me what it could mean. I kicked the donkey into a furious gallop and thundered into the monastery forecourt. The prior was waiting and I knew from his face that it was too late. Three hours earlier, Hugolino had been found lying in his garden with a dagger driven firmly between his shoulder-blades, whilst his murderer had vanished as quietly as he had come. Because of the intense heat, the good brothers had already dressed the body for burial and it lay in a wooden coffin before the altar of the monastery chapel. The prior wanted to know if I knew why Hugolino had been murdered, but I said nothing. I merely went and knelt beside the coffin and prayed for the king I had come to love and respect.

The next morning, he was buried beneath the chapel floor. The prior simply ordered the name "Hugolino" to be scratched on the flagstone and, although he looked very confused, he did not interfere when I added the word "Rex."

So, Richard, Edward the king is dead, and his bastard successor can live in peace. But can you, Richard? Why did you betray me? Only you, my friend, could have told the king where I was and what I had found. When did you betray me, Richard? From the beginning, and for what? What were your thirty pieces of silver? An abbey? A bishopric? May God forgive you, Richard, because I cannot. Nor will the king. I know I could be writing to a dead man. Perhaps he will intercept this letter. I hope so. Like any good clerk, I have made a copy of every letter I have sent you. I was always, if anything, an efficient, capable Chancery clerk. I will entrust these copies to capable hands. So the truth about our bastard king will never die.

This evening, my dear Judas, I am going to ride out of St Albert's and I know that I might never finish that journey. Like Hugolino, I too, must disappear. I am not afraid to die. I have lost all, and there is nothing left to live for. But before I finish, let me remind you, Richard, that you, not Guerney, nor Maltravers, nor Ockle, killed a king.
Written at Butrio, 15 February 1347.

Epilogue

In the name of the Father, and of the Son, and of the Holy Ghost, amen. I, Giuseppe, Abbot of the Monastery of St Albert at Butrio, have read all the above letters written by one Edmund Beche, English clerk, to Richard Bliton, Prior of the Abbey of Croyland. I cannot swear to the veracity of all they contain but only to the incidents which occurred at our monastery in the winter of 1347. I find it hard to accept that Hugolino, a common gardener, was the deposed Edward II of England. However, in a world where the King of Kings was a Jewish carpenter, anything can be true.

Master Edmund stayed a month at our monastery after his friend's murder. He merely tended the garden as Hugolino did and then one evening slipped quietly out of the monastery. I do not think that he resigned himself to death. That same evening, our brothers heard the sound of fighting far up the valley slope. The next morning a fair-haired *Inglese,* bleeding his life out, was found outside the great gate. Brother Giacommo, our infirmarian, did what he could but the unfortunate man died within the day. We searched his belongings for a name and found him to be Sir John Chandos, knight, baronet and a member of the household of Edward of England. In view of what Beche had written concerning this man, I decided to have him buried in unconsecrated ground, and the whole community has sworn an oath of secrecy never to reveal any information about his death. Since Beche's disappearance, English "envoys" on their way to Rome, or the court of the Two Sicilies, have frequently visited our monastery "on pilgrimage" or "to rest." I know their true intentions do not correspond to their open declarations, but none of them have left any the wiser for their visit.

The news I receive from our English brethren tells me that Queen Isabella still lives whilst her son wages terrible war in France. Prior Richard Bliton, however, has not been so fortunate, for he died from a strange sickness on his way to Rome. As for Beche himself, nothing has been heard. He may have escaped, for we scoured the hillsides and found no trace of him. Wherever he may be, I wish him peace, for he was a good, conscientious clerk who fought a good fight and finished the task assigned to him. His letters will be left for posterity.

Historical Note

History is full of strange mysteries and the death of Edward II must be reckoned one of the strangest. Many of the incidents described in the Butrio Manuscript are correct. Mortimer and Isabella were lovers. According to the French chronicler, Froissart, the queen was pregnant by Mortimer when the latter fell from power in 1330. Edward II was imprisoned at Berkeley Castle and Dunheved did go to Rome to seek a divorce and did launch a surprise attack on the castle to free his imprisoned master. History says he failed, but the Fieschi letter still exists to suggest the opposite. The fate of Edward II's purported murderers is obscure: Guerney was apprehended in Italy but died on his way back to England. Ockle disappeared for ever, but John Maltravers was given a pardon and served as Edward III's emissary in Flanders. Other items of information can also be verified: Isabella did have her "husband's" heart sent to her; she did hire an old woman to dress the corpse; Bishop Orleton was accused of sending that message to Edward II's gaolers; Mortimer did refuse to let the body be buried at Westminster and he did trick Edmund, Earl of Kent, into treason and summary execution.

Queen Isabella died in 1358 but Beche's curse on Edward III and his descendants did prove to be correct. The king's war with France finally turned into disaster. Edward III slipped into dotage, totally dependent on an unscrupulous mistress, Alice Perrers, who stayed beside his deserted deathbed only long enough to strip his corpse. Edward III's eldest son, the Black Prince, died of a terrible wasting sickness. His grandson, Richard II, was deposed and murdered in 1399. The crown of England passed into other hands.